HOPE
MOUNTAIN

Other Books by Jon Land

*Indicates a Forge Book

JON LAND

HOPE
MOUNTAIN

A TOM DOHERTY ASSOCIATES BOOK
NEW YORK

This is a work of fiction. All the characters and events portrayed in this novel are either fictitious or are used fictitiously.

HOPE MOUNTAIN

Copyright © 1998 by Jon Land

All rights reserved, including the right to reproduce this book, or portions thereof, in any form.

This book is printed on acid-free paper.

A Forge Book
Published by Tom Doherty Associates, Inc.
175 Fifth Avenue
New York, NY 10010

Forge® is a registered trademark of Tom Doherty Associates, Inc.

Design by Lynn Newmark

Library of Congress Cataloging–in–Publication Data

Land, Jon.
  Hope Mountain / Jon Land.—1st ed.
    p.   cm.
  "A Forge book"—T.p. verso.
  ISBN 0-312-86772-7
  I. Title.
  PS3562.A469H66 1998
  813'.54—dc21   98-21313
                                              CIP

First Edition: December 1998

Printed in the United States of America

0 9 8 7 6 5 4 3 2 1

For the staff and students
of the White Mountain Adaptive Ski School:

Heroes all.

ACKNOWLEDGMENTS

Thanks to . . .

Jamie Brandon, who gave me the idea.

Mary Lane, who helped flesh it out the same way she teaches: patiently.

Tim Lukens and Stu Kiely, who read it as both friends and experts.

Chuck Flanagan, who provided emergency medicine expertise.

Toni Mendez, who believed I could do it all along.

Natalia Aponte, who refused to settle for anything but my best, and touched every page.

Tom, Linda, and the whole Tor/Forge family, who saw a book here from the start.

Ann Maurer, who helped make it a book.

Bill Letezia, who came up with the title and the workout.

And finally, Ken Watson, who somehow taught me how to ski. See you next season, Ken! That's a promise.

"If I can do this, I can do anything."

Motto of Disabled Sports/USA

ONE

CHAPTER ONE

"How long has this been going on?"

Jen turned toward her brother in the Jeep's passenger seat.

"I want an answer, all right?" Matt continued, sounding considerably older than his fifteen years.

Jen swung back to the road and glimpsed the red light above her. She hit the brakes and heard the grinding screech in the last instant before the eighteen-wheeler barreled through the intersection and struck the Jeep Cherokee broadside. It spun across the road like a top, twisting and turning until the passenger side wrapped around a telephone pole in a shower of glass and steel.

Jen didn't remember much after that. There was the blistering bang of the air bag inflating, followed by the taste of blood in her mouth and the odd feeling that her teeth seemed to have shifted. Her vision was blurred and her head ached horribly. It hurt to breathe and something heavy was pressing against her chest. She managed to look down and saw that the heavy object was the steering wheel wrapped in the billowy shape of the deflated air bag.

I'm trapped. . . .

Regaining awareness was like being reluctantly stirred from a deep sleep. She fought it every step of the way, preferring the dark to the reality around her.

A soft moan drew her gaze to the passenger seat. For an instant she saw no one and was disoriented enough to believe she had been alone in the car. Then she glimpsed her brother Matt slumped against the seat back, shrouded from the face down by the floppy remnants of the air bag on the passenger side.

There were people at the smashed-in window on the driver's side by then, urging her to stay calm, not to move. But Jen tried to shimmy herself free and stopped when a surge of agony like hot lightning cut into her pelvis. She shrieked in pain and a man by the window smashed the remaining glass aside and plunged his hand through to press against her shoulder.

"Let go of me!"

"Don't move. Please. You shouldn't move."

"My brother! Help my brother!"

Jen thrashed to free herself, groping futilely toward Matt, coming up short. More hands jabbed through the window to hold her down. Jen fought them and her pelvis exploded in pain again.

The sound of sirens came next, picking up cadence as they drew closer. Jen closed her eyes, and when she opened them the firemen were surrounding the Jeep. The hands upon her now were those of paramedics. One of them spoke comfortingly to her before trying to cover her face with something heavy. Jen flailed and stripped it free. A fireman angled a Jaws of Life apparatus that looked like a huge pair of mechanical pliers to Matt's side of the Jeep. Once again the hands joined in against her. Jen's face and body were covered again and the rest of her held firmly in place.

The sound followed while she continued to struggle, a sound like an engine idling followed by a quick rev and a *pop!* as the Jaws of Life separated the passenger door from the Jeep's frame. The hands restraining her let up enough for Jen to shake free of her hood in time to see a flurry of hands easing Matt out from beneath what had been the dashboard. A brief surge of relief filled her until she saw the blood. It was everywhere, the seat soaked and darkened by it. As the paramedics held Matt still and attached a collar to his neck, more of it flooded from him in huge rivulets to the Jeep's floor.

Jen screamed.

"Hold her still!" one of the paramedics ordered, continuing his examination of Matt, stopping when he came to one of the boy's legs. Jen could see him hesitate then. Her eyes flashed downward and caught a glimpse of her brother's shredded jeans matted with blood.

"I need a leg splint here!" the lead paramedic ordered, and another scrambled to get it.

A wave of nausea struck Jen and then her view was blocked by the paramedic who had come back with the leg splint.

The man's eyes gaped as he helped steady Matt's leg. "God, he's lost a lot of blood. . . ."

"Keep your damn voice down!"

"We can't move him like this."

"The hell we can't!"

The chief paramedic worked furiously, barking orders as he immobilized Matt's leg. Whatever he was doing was out of Jen's line of vision, adding to her sense of helplessness.

What's going on? Jen wanted to ask. *What's happening?*

But the words choked up in her throat. She could barely swallow.

"This one's stable!" a voice near her roared, and only then did Jen realize other paramedics had been working on her as well.

"Matt!" she managed to scream finally, and the men looked at each other from across the twisted remnants of the front seat.

"Okay," said the paramedic working on Matt, "we're going to move him."

"Christ," from another, shaking his head.

More hands pushed their way in toward Matt.

"On my mark. One, two, *three!*"

The hands worked in unison and Matt glided gently outward, a trail of blood left dripping in his wake as the paramedics eased him toward the sunlight. Jen gagged and felt bile spill up into her throat. She swallowed it down and managed to shift enough to see four of the hands holding Matt's splinted leg like it was precious china. The acrid, coppery stench of blood filled the cab, as the hands lowered him to the pavement out of her sight line.

"Vitals strong!" a voice blared from over her.

"Blood pressure 170 over 110!"

"Strong breath sounds!"

"Let's get the Jaws over here!"

This last command uttered while an oxygen mask was lowered toward Matt.

"What are they doing? What's going on?"

"Try to relax," a voice soothed.

"I want to see my brother!"

She watched the paramedics working over him with frantic precision, readying IV pouches and lowering needles into that nether region below the Jeep's passenger-side running board. She could see their upper bodies and uniforms splattered with Matt's blood, latex gloves dripping with red too.

One of the paramedics shielded Jen's face with his coat. Then the low groan of the idling hydraulic pump for the Jaws of Life turned to a soft rumble as the machine separated steel. She heard her door bang to the pavement and then felt hands probing about her belly and hips.

"Okay," a voice said in her ear, trying to sound soothing, "we need to fit this collar on you."

The paramedic lifted the coat from her face and Jen turned her eyes back toward Matt. "I'm all right."

"I need you to turn to the front."

"I want to watch my brother."

"Your brother's doing well. He's stable. We need to get you out now."

Jen might have continued her protest if the paramedics on the other side of the Jeep hadn't hoisted Matt's spinal board gently upward and moved it toward a waiting ambulance.

"Hold still."

The next moment Jen felt the collar being clamped into place around her neck, keeping her head fixed so she couldn't turn it.

"Okay, let's get her out."

She fixed her gaze downward, afraid of the sight that awaited her as the paramedics eased her legs out from under the dashboard.

CHAPTER TWO

"What'll you have?"

Jamie Brooks looked up at the bartender and raked his fingers through his long, snow-dampened hair.

"Beer."

"What kind?"

"Draft. The cheapest you've got."

As the bartender turned to fill his order, Jamie rested his elbows on the counter and blew into his frigid hands. Even the short distance from his car to the front door had left him shaking from the cold, brutal for this time of year even by New Hampshire standards. Beyond the horseshoe-shaped bar, all but a few of the booths were empty. Band equipment was stacked on a makeshift stage set before a partitioned dance floor, though Jamie figured the storm had kept even the musicians away tonight.

"Here you go," the bartender said, setting a frosty mug down before him.

Jamie yanked a bill from his jeans and thrust it on the bar. He had guzzled almost half the beer when he heard the man's voice again.

"Ah, excuse me."

Jamie peered over the top of his mug.

The bartender was holding the bill Jamie had laid down. "What exactly do you call this?"

Jamie looked closer and saw that he had paid him with the eviction notice he had plucked from his apartment door ten hours earlier. He quickly reached into his pocket for a real bill to replace it.

"Sorry."

"Sure," the bartender said, and readjusted the duckbill baseball cap that cast a thin shadow down the length of his face. In spite of the weather, he was wearing a short-sleeve shirt and his biceps looked like baseballs squeezed under his skin.

Jamie crunched the eviction notice in his fist and deposited it in the nearest ashtray atop the shiny, light-finished wood. He snatched a book of matches someone had left on the bar, struck one, and touched the flame to the balled-up paper.

He had found the notice taped to his door by his landlord Mrs. Dellagash just before the first time he almost died that day. Crumpled it up and stuffed it in the same pocket as his few remaining dollar bills. The bills were the last of his savings, even fewer since he had stopped at the drugstore early that morning.

When he got back to the apartment, Jamie had gone straight into the small kitchen, smelling the scent of Meg strongly for a moment. He knew from experience that for some reason he didn't understand, her scent would fade away in a few minutes. The first days without her he had made excuses to go out, found errands to run just so he could come back and feel Meg near him. Each time he returned her scent was fainter, the time when it would fade forever inevitable.

But he wasn't going to wait for that day to come.

The pills in the prescription bottle clinked against each other as he set the CVS bag down on the kitchen table in the same spot where he'd found Meg's note the week before.

It's not working out. . . .

The note said more, but that was the line Jamie kept coming back to. They had been going out since high school and things had *always* worked out. They had gotten through everything until now, so what had changed?

Jamie considered that question again as he shifted the CVS bag onto a place mat. The pills inside were like a legacy. His leg had hurt for years after the accident, a painkiller called Vicoden the only thing that could calm it while casting a deep dreamlike blur over the world.

It had been five years since Jamie had gotten his last prescription, just before his nineteenth birthday. But he'd never had it filled, a recollection that had sent him scurrying out the night before to scavenge through his glove compartment as though there were treasure to be found. He'd about given up hope when a shake of the owner's manual sent the small sheet of scribble fluttering out, wrinkled and a little faded, yet reasonably intact. Altering the year at the prescription's top was as simple as changing a "3" to an "8."

Jamie stripped his jacket off and laid it over the back of a chair. Then he snatched up the CVS bag and walked the length of the apartment into the bathroom, where he made sure to pull the shade down all the way before turning on the twin faucets of the tub. He adjusted the water temperature, then stood back up and removed the Vicoden from the CVS bag. He had trouble working the child-guard cap, but finally popped it off and tipped a half-dozen pills into his palm, gulping them down with a swig from the tap.

The water ballooned his jeans as he sank into the tub and settled back. He remembered he had left the razor blades on the vanity and reached up to snag them from inside the CVS bag. The Vicoden was starting to work now, a dull fog misting over reality the way the steam covered the mirror.

Jamie pulled the top blade from the package and threw

out the rest. He lowered the steel edge to his wrist and shuddered at its cold touch, closing his eyes to concentrate on Meg's fading scent, imagining her hair bouncing behind her as she lugged her suitcases toward the door, just before he felt himself drifting, drifting away. . . .

CHAPTER THREE

"Do you always see patients at night?"

As she spoke, Jen kept her stare fixed out the window into the spill of a flickering streetlight. A light rain had begun to fall, speckling the glass.

"Only when they call me," Dr. Ryerson said and crossed her legs.

"This is only my second visit."

"All the more reason. What happened after they got you out of the Jeep?"

"They took Matt and me to the hospital. Separate ambulances. I wasn't hurt badly. A few cuts and bruises, that's all."

Dr. Ryerson made a note on the pad before her, visible to Jen as a reflection in the darkened, water-flecked glass, a reflection infinitely preferable to her own. Jen looked years older, although only a week had passed since the accident. Her face was pale and drawn. Tiny lines had formed around her mouth.

"How old is your brother, Jen?"

She turned from the window and faced Dr. Ryerson. "Isn't that in the history I wrote out last time?"

"I'd prefer to hear it from you."

"Fifteen."

"And how old are you?"

"Twenty-eight next week. Should I sit down?"

"That's up to you."

Jen moved to the chair opposite Dr. Ryerson, but didn't sit down. The simplicity of the office surprised her. The leather love seat and chairs were arranged comfortably around a gas fireplace aglow with a soft orange flame. A rose-colored oriental rug, sun-bleached along the far edge, covered the floor in front of an uncluttered Queen Anne desk. During her first visit, Jen had noticed a series of framed pictures atop it,—Dr. Ryerson's husband and children, she guessed. The only one picturing the doctor herself featured her in midflight down a ski slope, catching her in the midst of a turn. Jen thought it must have been taken fairly recently.

She looked at the demure Ryerson now and tried to visualize her carving up snow on some black-diamond trail. Just thinking about it made her pelvis ache; not a serious injury, the doctors had assured her, but a lingering one all the same that had kept her from her regular six-mile runs.

"You and Matt have different fathers?" Dr. Ryerson asked.

"My father died when I was eleven. My mother remarried two years later. She was forty when Matt was born."

"And Matt's father?"

Jen stiffened a little. "He left three years ago."

"Was that after your mother . . ." Dr. Ryerson let her question tail off purposefully.

"No—before." Jen felt something hot building in her face. "You shouldn't ask for a patient history if you're not going to read it."

The two women stared at each other for a long moment, the quiet ticking of a clock perched on the psychiatrist's ornate shelves the only sound between them. Finally Dr. Ryerson took pen in hand again.

"Let's talk about what happened after you got to the hospital."

*   *   *

*Jen climbed down off the narrow emergency-room bed
and slipped through a crack in the lime-colored curtain.
It hurt terribly to walk, the pain centered squarely in
the middle of her pelvis. Each step seemed to grind bone
together, but she kept moving deeper into the ER,
checking the various rooms and cubicles for Matt.*

*She found him in a trauma room in the center of
three beds, surrounded by doctors and nurses working
with grim determination. She moved closer, and they
seemed not to notice her.*

*Matt was blocked from her view mostly, but she
could see they had removed the splint applied by paramedics at the scene and cut away the jeans to expose his
shattered leg. Distance spared her full view of the damage; she saw enough, though, to stagger her woozily
backward.*

*Below the knee, it didn't even resemble a leg any-
more, just a mishmash of flattened bone, gristle, and
muscle. They must have stopped the blood because the
exposed jagged husk of Matt's leg was a sickly pinkish
color now.*

*"Someone get her out of here!" a doctor finally or-
dered, and a pair of nurses moved toward Jen.*

*As they led away from the bed, she had a clearer
view of Matt and she saw that, ridiculously, his foot
looked totally intact.*

"Tommy Hilfiger," Jen finished.

"Who?" asked Dr. Ryerson.

"The kind of jeans Matt was wearing. Eighty-five dollars.
I remember buying them for him. I remember thinking how
upset he'd be to wake up and find them ruined."

"His leg . . ."

"I had to sign some papers. That was the hardest part. I

didn't want to make the decision alone. I wanted to talk to him. I needed time."

"And the doctors told you there wasn't any."

"Emphatically. They kept stressing they could save the knee. That was very important. The rest, well, I had seen for myself. That still didn't make it any easier."

"It never does."

"Accepting responsibility—that's what this comes down to. I'm holding the clipboard in front of me, everyone's waiting for me to sign, and I'm afraid of making another mistake. Doing the wrong thing. To this day I'm still not sure I didn't do the wrong thing. I mean, I could have waited, insisted they pursue other options."

"You said you had seen for yourself."

"That's not what I'm talking about. I *wanted* Matt to come live with me; nobody forced me to do it. But I'm not sure I ever accepted responsibility for him. I never understood exactly what that meant."

"Was there an alternative?"

"Not one that I could live with."

The clock ticked on.

"You think I did the right thing. . . ."

"No," said Dr. Ryerson. "I would have waited for the jeans to go on sale."

Jen tried to smile.

"Do you feel you did something you weren't ready for?"

"On-the-job training. We could have made it work; it was working." Jen heard her voice cracking. "Then I'm holding a clipboard and they're asking me to change everything forever."

"Again."

"I guess."

"So you accepted responsibility, as you told me."

"And ruined my brother's life in the process."

"Does Matt believe that or do you?"

"Both of us, I think." Jen managed to smile this time but there was something all wrong about it. "Last thing we have in common, you might say."

"If you had it to do all over again, you wouldn't sign the papers. Is that it?"

Jen was trembling now. "I wouldn't have run that damn red light. That's what. It was my fault. The whole goddamn thing was my fault and having to sign those papers was like going through it twice. I go to sleep at night and sometimes I see the traffic light and sometimes I see the papers. But I haven't gone back to that intersection. Even if it means going twenty minutes out of my way, I won't go back to that intersection."

"Did you contact Matt's father?"

"He was telling me how sorry he was when his call waiting clicked in. I hung up after hanging on for five minutes."

Dr. Ryerson's eyebrows flickered. "He never called back?"

"No."

"How did that make Matt feel?"

"Matt hates him anyway."

"And you?"

"I think Matt hates me now, too."

"I was asking you about Matt's father."

"Oh. Sorry."

"For what?"

"There are too many things to list."

"Start with the most important."

Jen took a deep breath. "I'm sorry I can't help Matt, that I can't reach him anymore, that maybe I've lost him for good."

"You said you wanted to talk more about the accident itself," Dr. Ryerson said. "What led up to it."

"The drugs. We were arguing about drugs. I found them in his jeans the night before."

"Did you confront him?"

"Not exactly," Jen said evasively.

Dr. Ryerson looked confused for the first time. "You *didn't* confront him?"

Jen finally sat down, but leaned forward stiffly. "I haven't told this to anyone yet."

"But it's the real reason why you called me tonight, isn't it?"

"Yes," Jen said softly.

"We've still got half the hour left."

Jen started speaking again, wondering if that would be long enough.

CHAPTER FOUR

"As a rule, we leave the charcoal broiling to the kitchen," the bartender said, eyeing the smoldering remnants of the eviction notice.

"They still cooking?"

He set Jamie's change down before him. "Don't know, given the hour."

"What time is it?"

"Ten-thirty."

Where had all the time gone?

The bartender looked at Jamie uneasily. "You want a menu?"

"Please."

The bartender moved off to grab one, picking up the ashtray and dropping it into a sink full of soapy water on his way.

"Order fast," he said, plopping a menu down atop Jamie's change. "They want to close up, get home before it really gets bad out there."

Jamie studied the menu as he finished his beer. He desperately wanted another but held back from ordering it, afraid of what more alcohol would do in concert with the Vicoden. His head had already begun to throb, the worst of the pangs making him feel nauseous.

Watching some of the beer suds slide over the glass's rim made Jamie think of the water pouring from the bathtub when he had burst up from it gagging earlier in the day. He gasped for breath and grabbed hold of the tub's sides to hoist himself upward before staggering out. Water cascaded off him, spilling out of his jeans and making straight for the wood floor beyond the bathroom.

The razor blade!

He checked his wrist for the neat vertical slice he'd intended to make but found nothing.

I must have passed out before drawing it across the vein, must have sunk under the water and almost drowned instead. . . .

Jamie slid to the tile floor, knees tight against his chest, and wrapped his arms around himself. His wet clothes sagged around him, oozing cold water. His hair was a wild tangle that smelled like fear.

He rested on the floor in a ball until his teeth stopped chattering, thought he might have passed out again but wasn't sure. He was still shivering when he pushed himself back up the wall. The steam had cleared from the mirror long ago and the sight of his face terrified him. A pale, bloodless visage that looked like his father's had looked caked with makeup in his coffin.

Jamie's clothes squished as he moved from the bathroom, his bare feet leaving wet footprints on the wood. Outside dusk had fallen and he could hear traffic on the street beyond.

Dusk . . .

Three hours had passed since he had stepped into the tub, maybe four. Still freezing, he walked to the living room radiator and cranked the valve open all the way. The pipes rattled as steam hissed upward. Jamie sank against the old steel until his flesh burned and the shaking stopped. The room was turning dark by then and he could hear a television blaring in one of the neighboring apartments.

He stood up again and sloshed into the bedroom where he

turned on the light and yanked off his shirt. His jeans came next, discarded in a soggy pile to the floor. He found fresh clothes in his closet and put them on without drying himself completely. The jeans clung to his thighs as a result, and the shirt felt clammy against his skin.

What now?

In forming his desperate plan, Jamie had at the time felt an eerie sense of resignation, if not contentment. Now he had to face himself again in the wake of yet another failure, the future a black ugly void hanging in his path. All he had left was forty-six dollars and his father's ten-year-old Saab, the contents of its glove compartment still scattered across the passenger seat. At least the gas tank was full, 350 miles of driving he could count on.

350 miles . . .

He drew a map in his mind to see where that might take him. Pick a direction and just drive until he ran out of gas and money. Then find a way to make enough to start driving again.

Why the hell not?

Turn around and do not look back. Go.

Jamie gazed back into the bathroom. The last of whatever still tied him here lay cooling with the bath water. He had forty-six dollars and a full tank of gas—enough to get him away, and away was where he wanted to be.

He felt his resolve returning. Saw himself behind the Saab's wheel, his past shrinking in the rearview mirror, heading . . .

Heading *where?*

North. North was all he really knew from his teenage years spent skiing every weekend at Okemo, or Stratton, or Sunday River, or Killington, or Loon where Cap Morgan had led the team that carried him down off the mountain after the accident eight years before.

Awkwardly, Jamie stuffed an old suitcase and a gym bag with as much as they could carry, a collection of clothes and possessions crammed in without reason or order. He took the gym bag in one hand, the suitcase in the other, and was halfway to the door before he remembered the forty-six dollars stuffed in his soaked jeans. Back in the bedroom, he drew the bills out in a clump and wedged them into the deep pocket of the baggier pair he had donned. Couldn't wait to get on the road.

The drive north from Rhode Island had passed easily at the outset, long hazy stretches broken only by the blare of a horn or sting of high beams in his rearview mirror. But the road stayed firm beneath the old Saab's tires, and the car's speed hovered around sixty until the intermittent swirls of snow began to thicken well past the New Hampshire border. The wipers battled them successfully at first, then began to cake up with ice, the streaks left on the windshield widening with each swipe.

Jamie tried crimping his neck to peer through the clear patches, but the snow quickly blanketed the road and obscured the lane markers. Route 93 was unlit and the brief glimpses he managed to snatch of the world beyond revealed the White Mountains rising ominously on all sides of him, great beasts ready to strike.

A horn screamed, catching Jamie in a weave between lanes. He worked the brake and the Saab fishtailed into a skid that brought him back across northbound traffic. He spun out into the path of headlights suddenly streaming straight at him. Jamie felt the snow crunching beneath his tires, closed his eyes as he skidded sideways with his wheels locked up and the cars coming dead on.

He opened his eyes again after the Saab had stopped moving and saw that it was facing the wrong way in the breakdown lane, its rear end perched precariously on the shoulder.

Jamie took a deep breath. Waited until there were no oncoming lights in view before easing the Saab back onto the road in a sweeping half circle. Then he clung to the breakdown lane and crept toward the promise of an exit a half-mile ahead.

Jamie veered off and tried his high beams but the snow just bounced them back, leaving him only the trail of another car's ruts to keep from straying off the ramp. He coaxed the car right at the ramp's end and found himself mired in a long, dark tunnel. A half-mile up a plow came barreling at him, a mountain of snow pushed before it, and Jamie swung right toward the lights of a well-lit road. He continued on until his wipers got the windshield clear again, then swerved into the parking lot of a restaurant called Woodstock Station, straddling a pair of spaces as he skidded to a halt.

When was the last time I ate?

The thought had sent Jamie back to the menu when he felt a hand grab his shoulder.

"Jesus Christ, it *is* you! I don't believe it!"

Jamie turned toward the strangely familiar voice, and Cap Morgan wrapped him in a bear hug that brought him down off the stool and into his waiting arms.

CHAPTER FIVE

Jen returned home to find five messages on her answering machine, four of them from her supervisor in the district attorney's office. He had beeped her repeatedly through the evening until she had finally switched the damn thing off before going to Dr. Ryerson's office, tired of the chirping sound and his office number displayed angrily in the window.

"Jen, it's Chuck Woodley. I'm at the office call me."

"Jen, it's Chuck again. We need to talk."

"Jen, this is for your own damn good. If you don't call back, I can't be responsible for what happens."

"Last chance, Jen."

The fifth call was from the nursing home, a new night-shift attendant with the same questions all first-timers called her with.

"My, you're a pretty young lady," her mother had said from her bed when Jen arrived that afternoon, a television talk show droning in the background. "What's your name?"

"Jen."

"Nice name. Do you know mine?"

"It's Fran."

She got that puzzled look on her face that always quickly gave way to fear. "No, I don't think that's it at all. . . ."

Jen reached out and took her hand. "I brought things to show you."

"What . . . things?"

"Pictures."

"Pictures of what?"

"People mostly."

"I think I'd rather watch television. Turn it on."

Jen pretended to flip the switch on the set already playing.

"That's better," her mother sighed. "Have I had my lunch yet?"

"Yes."

Jen lifted a photo album from the bedside night table.

"What's that?" her mother asked her.

"Pictures."

"Can I see them?"

"Sure."

As always, Jen set the album before her mother and turned the pages when Jen sensed she was ready. In those moments, even when she didn't express it, the woman who had been her mother came to life as memories captured by Kodak and Polaroid flipped past her. Occasionally unfelt tears would slide down her cheeks, remaining there until Jen dabbed them.

"Your father was here last night," her mother said suddenly. "He looked tired. He works too hard." She grabbed Jen's arm in a burst of intensity. "How's school?"

"Good."

"I signed your report card. It's on the kitchen table."

"Thank you."

"You promise to do better next term?"

"Yes."

She nodded and pulled her hand away. "I'll tell your father not to worry." Then, just like that, her eyes sharpened. "Jenny?"

"Hi, Mom," Jen said and felt a warm gush of relief sweep over her.

"I must have been sleeping. How long have you been here?"

"Just walked through the door."

"Hungry? I could have them bring you something. . . ." Her mother gazed about the room anxiously, suddenly not seeming to recognize it.

"It's all right. I'm fine."

Her mother looked back at the photo album and came to a picture of Matt in a soccer uniform from two years before, just before the first signs of her Alzheimer's had appeared.

"Did Matt come with you today?"

"No, Mom, not today."

"What about you? You look tired."

Jen felt something like a dam break deep inside her. "I'm in trouble, Mom." It felt so good saying that, having someone to talk to for a few minutes anyway. But her mother wouldn't remember her words tomorrow, or even in an hour, and Jen wondered if that made it easier to tell her.

"Trouble?"

She saw the concern flicker in her mother's eyes and wanted to cling to the moment for as long as she could. "I think I'm going to lose my job."

"That's ridiculous. You're the best lawyer they've got."

"I made some mistakes. It all got to be too much and things got away from me." Jen looked into her mother's eyes and longed for the person she remembered. "I could go to jail."

"You'd better talk to your father about this. You'd . . ." The words bottlenecked and quickly turned into a slur. Then her lips kept moving and nothing emerged at all.

"Mom," Jen said, hoping she could lure her back. "Mom?"

Something like recognition, awareness, flickered in her mother's still-bright eyes. Then fear, and remembrance perhaps, replaced it until her entire expression grew distant and

Jen knew she was far away again. Able to flip through the pages of the scrapbook slowly with a smile frozen on her lips, but that was all.

She sat down in the chair at the bedside. Her mother's moments of lucidity were few and far between as it was, but soon they would become nonexistent. Soon the small gifts of remembrance, however blurred, would vanish forever behind a curtain Jen would be powerless to part.

The fact that they had always been so close made the sudden onset of the disease doubly devastating. Her mother was so young they had both passed off the initial symptoms to simple absentmindedness. Only when her mother had taken over an hour to find her way home from a supermarket in town had they both realized something was terribly wrong.

Jen had not yet told her mother about the accident, everything else but not that, because she didn't know how. Jen kept making excuses for Matt's continued absence in those brief moments when her mother asked about him. Knowing she'd just forget anyway, which meant Jen would have to tell the story again and again. Not telling it at all seemed infinitely preferable.

From the chair, Jen watched her mother flipping the pages of the photo album randomly now. Then, suddenly, she jabbed a finger at a picture and angled the book toward Jen. "This is you, isn't it?"

The picture was more than a dozen years old, showed Jen around Matt's age, in braces, and yet her mother had recognized her, made the connection.

"Yes."

In that moment she was her mother again. But before Jen could seize the instant, her finger strayed to another face. "And who's this?"

Jen tried not to look as sad as she felt. "My mother."

"And this?" her mother asked, pointing to the last picture

of Matt taken before the accident. He was wearing the same jeans she had seen cut away in the emergency room.

Jen was about to speak when she saw her mother had drifted off to sleep, the photo album containing the lost memories of her life left open on her lap.

CHAPTER SIX

"You picked a fine night to take a drive, son," Cap said, holding Jamie's shoulders at arm's distance.

Jamie brushed a sleeve against his eyes. "Am I dreaming, or is it really you, Cap?"

"In the flesh." Cap tapped his stomach. "A little more of it since the last time I saw you."

"How far are we from Loon?"

"Three miles."

"This is *Lincoln?*" Jamie asked, not believing where fortune had deposited him in the storm.

"Woodstock, actually. Smack dab on Route 3." Cap leaned forward. "If you don't mind me saying, you don't look so good."

He had said the very same thing as the emergency crew lifted Jamie out of the thick cushion of snow eight years before. Jamie had gotten incredible air, ten or fifteen feet of it, but something had gone wrong with his landing. His ski tips had come up too far and he had tumbled headlong over and over again, coming to rest in a blanket of snow that felt warm when it shouldn't have.

"Lift on my count: one, two . . . three!"

Tom Morgan, his ski coach, whom everyone called "Captain" after the rum that was popular among high schoolers that year, stood over him watching the Loon Mountain ski patrol ease his stretcher into the Snowcat. Trying to hide his concern behind a fake smile.

"Guess I screwed up," Jamie managed to say.

"I warned you to stay away, didn't I, son? The Chute's chewed up better skiers than you." Cap was only around thirty then, but he had still called him 'son.' "Chewed 'em up and spit 'em out."

"How bad?" Jamie had asked after Cap climbed into the Snowcat to accompany him down the mountain.

Cap had glanced grimly at the thick padding the emergency team had fastened around Jamie's leg to immobilize it. "We'll see."

Jamie had won the under-eighteen championships the weekend before and was getting ready for the regionals. Feeling invincible, he had taken on the Chute, the only New England opponent he hadn't bested. The Chute wasn't a real trail, not in the sanctioned sense anyway. It wasn't listed on any map, and most of those who came to Loon looking for it went away disappointed. The Chute had formed over the remnants of an old waterfall on Loon's south mountain, land that belonged to the United States Forest Service. There were no lift towers, no snow guns, no patient grooming by Snowcats. Just an icy, twisting slope cut between rocks and trees that would have been a double black diamond if it were ever opened for real.

The early part of the trail had left him wanting to scream with delight. He was riding its bend, working his hips ahead of the breaks. Trees whistled by, their wind-rustled branches applauding him. He could feel the hammering of his heart settle as he became one with the mountain, owning the trail so it wouldn't own him.

He didn't know where he caught air, or how he caught so much of it. Even then, Jamie had thought he had positioned himself perfectly to land, accounting for everything but the icy patch that at his pace was like an oil slick on a race track. He was rolling before he realized it, sucking snow as he tried to scream. Ended up on his back coughing it from his mouth.

Jamie didn't know how long he had lain there before Cap found him several minutes ahead of the ski patrol's arrival.

"I can't feel my leg," he realized in the back of the Snow-cat.

Cap reached out and squeezed his hand. "It's still there."

"You're supposed to say you've seen worse. That's what you're supposed to say."

"You just worry about getting ready for the regionals. You hear me?"

Now, as Cap sat down in a chair across from him at a table in a dining room adjacent to the Woodstock Station bar, Jamie compared him to the man he had known eight years ago. His light curly hair was cut a bit shorter now and the crow's feet under his eyes had dug their way in deeper. His complexion showed a few more creases from too much exposure to the harsh winter sun and wind. Other than that, though, he could have been exactly the same man who had tried to coach Jamie to the Olympics.

"I can't believe you're still up here," Jamie said.

Cap took a swig from his beer. "Where else would I be?"

"Director of skiing?"

"Technical director. Suits me just fine." Another swig. "Should I ask how you're doing?"

"Not unless you want me to tell you."

"Consider the question asked."

"I'm here, aren't I?"

"That it?"

"Consider the question answered."

Cap looked across the table, studying Jamie's eyes. He frowned his displeasure. "Booze?"

"Vicoden."

"You still taking them for pain?"

"Six will dull just about anything."

A waitress appeared from the kitchen and set Jamie's hamburger and fries down before him. The fries were greasy and the burger had been grilled by someone in a hurry to leave, rare through and through. But Jamie doused it with ketchup and chomped into it gratefully, unable to recall a time when food had tasted so good. He noticed a clutter of hastily scrawled notes had been squeezed beneath the glass tabletop and began to read them as he chewed. Wondered what he would write, if he decided to leave one himself.

"Seriously," Cap said. Jamie shifted his plate to finish an especially long note. "How's the leg?"

"Good days and bad. More good, as time's gone on."

"You listen to the doctors and stay off the slopes?"

"I go slow."

"You and slow are words I never heard mentioned in the same sentence."

"Times change."

"So it seems. You got a place to stay?"

"I was thinking about my car," Jamie said between mouthfuls.

Cap looked out the window. "Not the best weather for it."

"I was thinking about that, too."

"What the hell you doing up here, son?"

"I don't know, Cap. That's the truth. I'd tell you if I did."

Cap's gaze drifted toward the window again. "Gonna be a great weekend for skiing. The mountain'll be packed."

"Good for business."

"Yeah," Cap said, the word dissolving into a deep sigh. "Damn . . ."

"What?"

"Here we are, sitting in a bar in the middle of a blizzard after, what, five years . . ."

"Closer to six."

". . . and the best I can do is make small talk." Cap leaned back in the booth. "I heard about your dad. Sorry I missed the funeral."

"No need to apologize."

"I should've kept in touch. It just slipped away from me."

"I missed you too, Cap," Jamie said, wolfing down the last of his burger and going to work on the fries.

"You want another beer?"

"A soda'd be fine."

"Good choice," Cap said, and yelled his order to the waitress he knew by name. "How'd it happen? Your dad, I mean."

"Heart attack."

"Shit."

"That's the way he felt. It's supposed to get easier as you get older but it got harder for him, a lot harder. Unjust, unfair—I could go on."

"Don't let me stop you," Cap said, rolling his bottle of beer between his hands as the waitress brought Jamie a Coke.

"No. I've said enough."

Cap caught the look in Jamie's eyes and let it go. "I let you down, son."

"You wrote some letters. I could have written back."

"What about your girlfriend? How's she doing?"

"She moved back in with her parents. I haven't written her either."

Cap shook his head slowly. "Anything going right you want to tell me about?"

Jamie cleaned the last of the fries off his plate. "I made it here. You found me."

"You'll stay at my place tonight."

"Thanks."

"What happens tomorrow?"

"I haven't thought that far ahead yet."

Cap cast him a sidelong glance, eyes flashing. "You mean what you said before, that you still know your way around a pair of skis?"

Jamie thought about the few times he gone up with Meg. The kids flying past, or whizzing along on more difficult slopes nearby. His eyes followed them and his guts would begin to ache, feeling as chewed up as the leg, which worked well enough but could snap again at any time if pushed too hard.

"Not like the old days," he said.

"But put you on a trail, you can find your way down."

"I guess," Jamie nodded, half lying since the doctor at his last orthopedic checkup had said there was no way he should try. But that was over two years ago. The leg felt much better now. "Why?"

"Just thinking, that's all. See, there's a position at Loon available. Might be just the right thing for an ex-champ like yourself who can work the slopes."

Jamie perked up. "Instructor?"

Cap didn't quite nod.

"Sounds too good to be true."

"It's not, son, believe me."

"Cap?"

"You'll see what I mean tomorrow."

TWO

"Rise and shine, son," Cap called the next morning, a Thursday. "There's eighteen inches of fresh powder to take some turns on."

Jamie turned into the couch's rear cushions and tightened the comforter around his shoulders.

Cap prodded him. "Come on, I wanna see what you got."

"What I've got is a headache," Jamie said, stirring. His mouth felt pasty, and he tried to remember where the apartment's bathroom was. He sat up suddenly. "My car . . ."

"Safe and sound. We'll pick it up later."

Jamie tried to rub the life back into his face. He smelled coffee brewing. Outside the den window of Cap's apartment there was nothing but white.

"You want some eggs?"

"Sure."

Cap moved toward the galley kitchen, while Jamie dragged the comforter with him toward the bathroom, picking his way clumsily.

"Fried okay?" Cap asked him, after Jamie reemerged, his mouth still pasty but at least no longer feeling like cotton wool.

"Fine." Jamie guzzled some orange juice, then moved for the coffee in the hope that the caffeine rush might help his headache. "What'd you mean last night about a job? The instructor thing."

Cap cracked an egg and let it spill into the pan. "You really interested?"

"I don't have anywhere else I have to be."

Cap cracked a second egg, then a third. "Probably not the best thing for you right now. Just me shooting my damn mouth off."

The eggs were starting to sizzle. Jamie sat down at the table and turned his gaze out the window again.

"There's nothing I'd rather do right now than get back to skiing, Cap."

"This ain't skiing, son, not as you know it," Cap said, and plopped the three eggs on a plate he set in front of Jamie. Four slices of toast popped up and he moved to fetch them.

Jamie captured a forkful of eggs and raised it toward his mouth. "The sport change that much in the few years I've been away?"

Cap just looked at him. "Finish up your breakfast. There's someone I want you to meet."

"I'm not promising anything," Cap had said, when they got to the Governor Adams Base Lodge at Loon Mountain. "Even if you're right for this, there's no saying it'll be right for you."

"You wanna tell me what you're talking about, what the big mystery is?"

Normally the cold air and feel of a clear, crisp morning with an empty mountain of fresh powder to conquer was like magic for any seasoned skier. But Jamie just felt cold until they entered the lodge.

"The White Mountain Adaptive Ski School."

"The *what?*"

"Program that works with the disabled, people who used to be called handicapped."

"You planning on enrolling me?"

"That's not exactly what I had in mind. They lost an instructor last week. With training coming up, they need to replace him fast."

"What'd you tell them about me, Cap?"

"That you had lots of experience."

"Working with the disabled?"

"Skiing—that's all the experience you need for starters."

Jamie felt a little deflated, let down. "I don't know, Cap. . . ."

"It's not up to you anyway, son. People don't like what they see and hear, they'll be after me for just suggesting you." Cap led him down a corridor on the ground floor of the Governor Adams Base Lodge, stopping in front of an open double door. "Here we are. The mountain donates this space."

"In the basement," Jamie noted.

"No stairs, son," Cap said and ushered him inside.

The adaptive ski school's headquarters was empty right now, save for an older man wearing a carpenter's apron filing down something in a closet-sized workroom located to the right of the entrance. The headquarters consisted of an L-shaped room fronted by a pair of tables and a check in counter with a computer. Jamie could see a narrow hallway, lined with equipment on both sides, jutting out from the rear wall toward a door leading to the trails. There was a also a single inner office, empty right now with the lights off.

"You don't mind," Cap said, "I'm gonna squeeze in a few turns."

Jamie looked back at Cap, as the sound of a saw grinding replaced the noise of the file in the work room. "You're not gonna wait and introduce me?"

"You're expected," Cap said, and started for the door. "Good luck."

After he left, Jamie busied himself with a closer scrutiny of the walls, starting with the various pictures of what looked to be some of the program's students in action. He stopped when he came to a shot featuring more than forty men and women from college to middle age in matching jackets—instructors, he gathered—grouped around the red, white, and blue WELCOME TO LOON MOUNTAIN sign posted at the entrance off Route 112. Before the word MOUNTAIN, though, one of them was holding up a sign that obliterated LOON and replaced it with HOPE.

Jamie studied the faces of those pictured to see if he recognized anyone. He heard footsteps and turned to see a tiny woman, just over four feet tall, enter. She moved stiffly, wobbling from side to side on severely bowed legs. Jamie was just about to tell her the people in charge were expected back shortly when she snatched a red, white, and black instructor's jacket from one of the pegs.

"You Brooks?" she asked, as she pulled her arms through the sleeves.

"Uh . . ."

"That too tough a question for you?"

"I'm Brooks, yes. Jamie Brooks."

"I'm Marge. My friends call me Midge."

"Hi, Marge."

She stared up at him. "You my friend?"

"What?"

"Call me Midge. I'm giving you the benefit of the doubt."

"Midge."

"Good." She put her hands on her hips. "Now how much did Cap tell you about what we do here?"

"Nothing."

"Smart. Keeps you from forming any preconceived notions." Marge looked him over. "He pleaded a pretty strong case for you with me last night. Tell you the truth I'm not impressed. Ex-hotshot with no experience working with the disabled—what am I supposed to do, perform miracles?"

Jamie let his eyes roam across the framed pictures again. "Something you're no stranger to, apparently."

"Surprised?"

"I just didn't know people like that could ski."

Marge nodded emotionlessly. "Like that . . ."

"Sorry."

"For what?"

"Being disrespectful."

"You weren't being disrespectful, you were being human. Now, if you still talk that way when I'm done with you, *then* you'd be disrespectful and we won't be dancing together come the Harvest Ball."

"Agreed."

"There's no agree or disagree to it, Brooks, and that's the absolute most important thing you've got to realize about this place. The adaptive clients may come though that door in a wheelchair, on prostheses, with their guide dogs or their aides or their psychological dysfunctions. But once we get them on the slopes they're just like you and me; only the equipment's different. On the slopes, they're not handicapped or disabled. They're self-sufficient and they're moving on their own, and for a lot of them it's the only time they can. The minutes we give them on the slopes let them be everything they used to be, and sometimes never were." She paused, looked Jamie over again noncommittally. "Cap tells me you used to be a champion."

"Long time ago, eight years. Under-eighteens. I was sixteen."

"Quite an accomplishment. Thing is, ex-champions often get impatient with those among us who can't fly."

"My flying days are long gone."

"You wanna work for me, you gotta rethink everything you know. Start from scratch. You follow me on that?"

"Yoda couldn't have said it any better himself."

"Well, young Luke, I don't care if it takes the Force or a cattle prod, if you want to make it here you'd better realize you're not skiing for yourself in this program; you're skiing for your student, because without you, he or she stays by the fire." Marge's eyes darted to the group picture shot before the WELCOME TO HOPE MOUNTAIN sign. "You take a look at that yet?"

Jamie nodded.

"Group shot of our instructors last year. Notice two of them are in wheelchairs?"

"Yes."

"Sounds strange, doesn't it?"

"No."

"Why?"

"Because they must understand the students better than anyone."

"What makes you think you could understand the students, then?"

"I had a skiing accident myself eight years ago."

"Qualifies you to be an instructor, that what you figure?"

"Not at all."

"Good," Marge said, "because it doesn't. You hurt yourself skiing and want to work with people who ski because they hurt themselves somewhere else. Or were born with some birth defect: MS, cerebral palsy, spina bifida. See, your background's not right at all." Marge frowned and zipped up her instructor's jacket. "Trouble is, with our yearly training sessions starting this weekend, I need somebody fast and I've learned over the years to trust Cap's judgment. But he's going way out on a limb this time. You screw up, Brooks, I'll never let him live it down."

"I couldn't have that," Jamie said.

Marge nodded, loosening the slightest bit. "Okay, let's start with the equipment," she said, and moved down the narrow aisle that led to the outer door. Outriggers hung on one side of the wall, skis on the other. "Many of our students, most even, ski with equipment not much different from what you or I would use. But for those with more intensive needs . . ."

Outside, Marge popped the lock off the door to a wooden shed and led the way in.

"Basically there are three different models of specialized adaptive equipment." She stopped at the device that looked like a small canoe or kayak. "This is a sit-ski. We call it a Disney ride because the student doesn't have to do anything but enjoy himself. But, believe me, you don't know how great that can be for someone confined to a wheelchair, a bed, or a room. We run it tethered to the wrist of an instructor who controls its speed from the rear. Questions?"

"No."

"Number two," Marge said, stopping below the next device. "A bi-ski, called that because you have two skis mounted beneath this chair the student is strapped into. On the sides you can have fixed outriggers designed for the adaptive skier with limited balance."

She slid sideways again, treating the shed's wall like a blackboard. "Now, for advanced adaptive skiers with a full upper body and good balance, we've got this: a mono-ski. It's got a chair too, like the bi-ski, but only one ski mounted on the underside for more speed and maneuverability. The outriggers on this model are handheld, just like poles, so the student is in total command and, believe me, they can approach speeds on this baby at least equal to champions like your-self."

"Ex-champion," Jamie reminded.

"How many times have you skied since?"

"All out?"

"Yes."

"None."

"Because you were scared."

"I prefer to call it reluctant," Jamie said, leaving out the part about the doctor's orders.

"Good."

"Good?" Jamie echoed.

"It doesn't come easy for you; it hasn't in awhile. If it did, I probably wouldn't have agreed to give you this shot. But now I know you'll be able to relate and, since I have no idea how patient or sensitive you are, that's the only thing you've got going for you, I shit you not."

"Better than nothing."

"Time will tell. Come on."

Back inside the school's headquarters, Marge grabbed an odd-looking pair of jet-black goggles from the wall. She handed them to Jamie. "We're not allowed to use these any-more."

"You making an exception in my case?"

"That's right. Put them on."

"I can't see a thing," Jamie said, after he had obliged, the strap digging into the back of his head.

"That's the whole idea."

CHAPTER EIGHT

The cold Jamie had felt before vanished as soon as he stepped outside and was dwarfed by the mountain rising before him. He had forgotten how good it was to feel the crunch of snow beneath his boots, a pair of skis hoisted effortlessly over his shoulder. The air was crystally cold and the ice-blue sky seemed to crackle with each toss of the wind.

Marge had found a decent-enough pair of skis for Jamie to borrow, and hearing the distinctive *click* when he clamped his feet down into them chased the last of his headache away. He drank in the air as they skied off toward the rope pull that would take them to the top of Sarsaparilla, Loon's most basic teaching trail.

It was Thursday, and the storm had socked in southern New England and many of the Mid-Atlantic states, so the mountain was virtually deserted. Jamie and Marge found they had Sarsparilla all to themselves.

"Okay, put your goggles back on," she instructed.

Jamie fitted them uneasily over his face and felt the strap biting into the back of his head again.

"What now?" he asked, utterly sightless, leaning on his poles.

"Ski."

"What?"

"You heard me: ski."

Jamie glanced back toward Marge's voice.

"The slope's the other way, hotshot."

He turned around again, but even that slight motion disoriented him, left him unsure which way the trail headed.

"Welcome to the White Mountain Adaptive Ski School," Marge continued. "You're now experiencing it from the inside out. How's it feel?"

"You've made your point."

"No, I haven't; I'm just getting started. There's two ways to play this: either you listen to me and we reach the bottom safely, or you don't pay attention and you crash and burn. Clear?"

"Crystal."

"Now, a blind skier typically takes one instructor, with one or two extras on weekends for traffic control. No tether in this case. The guiding is strictly vocal. Normally I'd go over the commands before starting—"

"Another exception in my case?"

"It's your lucky day, hotshot. Let's start with, Go!"

Jamie pushed off with his poles, skiing very slowly, every nerve and muscle in his body locked up tight.

"Left," Marge guided. "Left, left . . . Hold!"

Jamie ground his skis to a halt.

"What are you doing?" she asked him.

"What you said. Stopping."

" 'Stop' means stop. 'Hold' means hold your direction. Now let's get started again."

Jamie pushed off his poles once more and continued down the slope, matching his movements to Marge's commands.

"Right . . . Right . . . That's better. Let it out a little now. Left . . . Hold . . . Hold . . . Good, much better."

Jamie fought the snow every inch of the way, his ankles and knees throbbing, his legs straining against his boots. It was getting harder to maneuver as he sank deeper into this world of darkness.

Suddenly he felt something crash into him, low at the legs. He'd played football for a year in high school, so the feeling of getting tackled was nothing new for him. But getting tackled unsuspectingly in the snow was unsettling indeed. He went down hard and ended up with a mouthful of icy powder. Twisting onto his back, he stripped off his blackout goggles.

Marge knelt aside him, looking none the worse for wear.

"I know you had a reason for doing that," Jamie said, spitting the snow from his mouth.

"You hear my last few commands?"

Jamie realized his mind had been wandering and he hadn't. He shook his head.

"You see where you are?"

Jamie saw that the fence line was a mere six feet away.

"You didn't listen to my instructions and came close to crashing as a result. On Sarsaparilla that might get you just a laugh. But on another trail it gets you a broken leg or worse."

Jamie sat up and brushed the snow from his hair and face. "What are you gonna do next, throw me off the chairlift?"

"Close," said Marge.

They stood facing each other at the bottom of the nearest chairlift, located almost directly in front of the Governor Adams Base Lodge. A sit-ski rested between them, dragged here across the snow from the shed outside the school headquarters.

"Pick it up," Marge ordered.

Jamie leaned over and tried to do just that, but he was barely able to budge it off the ground.

"Jesus," he moaned.

"They weigh thirty pounds empty. This one's been weighted to a hundred and fifty to simulate a skier being inside." Marge steadied the wobbling sit-ski with her boot. "Here's the thing, Brooks. Working the slopes is the easiest part of what we do and also the most fulfilling. But first we've got to get our students and their equipment to the top, then get everything rigged to boot."

Marge backed off, giving Jamie space.

"What I want you to do is load the sit-ski on the seat when the chairlift goes by."

Jamie tested the weight of the sit-ski again, checking its distribution, before hoisting it upward. He steadied it in line with the chair, miscalculated, stumbled, and got smacked by the next chair coming for his efforts. The sit-ski toppled from his grasp.

Marge was grinning. "Anything to say for yourself, Brooks?"

"Ouch."

"Pretty tough, right?"

"Yeah."

"That's because it takes two people to load a sit-ski, not one."

Jamie was flexing his fingers. "Why didn't you just tell me?"

"I wanted you to understand why. Here, everything's about teamwork. I wanted you to experience what happens when you forget that."

"I'll remember now."

There were only a few volunteer instructors, plus Marge and one other full-time director, who worked weekdays at the school. The number swelled to over forty on weekends and vacations during peak season. Even so, the program had trouble meeting the demand for slots and runs. In that sense, Marge explained, it had become a victim of its own amazing victories and successes, especially in financial terms. Both the bi- and mono-skis, just like regular skis, had to be custom fitted to assure optimum performance and safety. But the cost of such an apparatus could easily run to several thousand dollars, and many students simply couldn't afford the expense. That's when the old man known as Merlin, who Jamie had seen earlier in the closet-sized workshop, worked his magic by adapting and transforming equipment to fit individual needs.

Marge told him that the program relied heavily on donations and a few fund-raisers. The instructors were all volunteers, the regulars who lived locally making what money they could working in Lincoln, Woodstock, or somewhere else nearby.

A big, muscular ex-football player named Frank Rawley, for example, worked as a bouncer in a local bar. Rawley had first come to the program to fulfill a community service obligation imposed after a street fight earned him a suspended sentence for assault and disorderly conduct. That community service obligation had ended three years ago, but the massive Rawley hadn't missed a weekend since, opting to attend college at the nearby University of New Hampshire so he could continue to spend his winter weekends at Loon. He had graduated last year and had settled, temporarily at least, in the Lincoln area.

The program's two paraplegic instructors made for a study in contrasts. Jed Tremblay had been a champion skier until a collision with a tree at the age of twenty-two had left him paralyzed from the waist down. Barely missing a beat, Jed, now twenty-five, had become a champion mono-skier and had several records to his credit.

Gus Bocamper, in contrast, was a southerner who had never skied in his life before a forklift crushed his legs during a summer construction job. They had been amputated at the hips. Without enough left to attach worthwhile prosthetics, Gus had learned to make do with only his stumps. Once he got his first taste of the slopes at a similar adaptive program in Vail, there was no getting him off them. Vail, though, had no use for his services once he was ready, so Gus had come east to Loon, where he now spent his winters. Summers he spent on the marathon circuit, breaking his own wheelchair speed records. As a result, he had developed an upper body close in size to Frank Rawley's and could bench press well over two hundred pounds.

After Marge was finished with him, Gus and Jed introduced Jamie to the finer points of mono- and bi-skiing. By sunset of his first day he had tried out the two devices and found himself woefully lacking in ability to maneuver either one. The more advanced mono-ski, especially, was a study in frustration. He couldn't find his balance or make the outriggers work consistently, taking spill after spill into the soft, fresh powder.

Jed had finally given up and decided to show him how it was done. He needed help only to get strapped in and settled. Jamie watched in amazement as Jed maneuvered expertly through the snow. In those moments, Jed wasn't handicapped, wasn't crippled, wasn't disabled at all. On the slopes, with nothing to hold him back, he could move as he had moved before his accident.

Only when they gathered together at the school's headquarters just before sunset did Jamie realize that he had just spent his first day in longer than he could remember without dwelling on the problems that had turned his life into a slow walk through quicksand. Even his desperate plunge into the bathtub only one day before seemed like a distant memory. Lately, he hadn't wanted anything very much, but he found himself desperately wanting to stay at Loon.

"Not bad for your first day," Marge complimented.

"Meaning there's going to be a second?"

"Training clinics start Saturday. You've got some catching up to do."

Jamie had started to smile when he saw the harsh stare Marge was giving him.

"But make no mistake about it, Brooks, I'm going against my better judgment here. And if you mess up on my watch I will personally kick your ass off this mountain, I shit you not."

"Deal," said Jamie.

CHAPTER NINE

"Do you have any questions for this witness, Miss Harrington?" The judge leaned forward over the bench. "Miss Harrington?"

"I'm sorry, Your Honor," Jen said. "No questions."

"In that case, we'll adjourn for the day and pick up again on Monday."

The gavel struck and Jen rose awkwardly to her feet. She'd managed to go through the motions again, but it was getting harder. Not that anyone noticed. The caseload of the typical Boston assistant district attorney was so great that it was easy to coast, but it was also supposed to be the best experience a fledgling criminal defense lawyer could get. Learn the office's weaknesses so when you're sitting at the opposite table you understand exactly what you're up against.

Things she used to care about.

Today she was supposed to be prosecuting a man accused of selling stolen merchandise to an undercover police officer. It was his third offense, virtually mandating a prison term if he were found guilty. But he had a wife and two kids, and a five year stretch in jail for him wasn't going to do them any good. Jen had wanted to offer a suspended sentence and probation in exchange for a plea bargain, but her office hadn't gone for it, insisting that examples needed to be made and wondering quietly behind Jen's back whether she was going soft.

Well, soft wasn't the word she would have used to describe it; more like obsessed. She could gaze around the courtroom and go into detail about the families of all the participants. The judge had just become a grandfather for the third time, the bailiff was working two jobs to put his daughter through college, the defendant's lawyer was divorced and saw his kids only on alternate weekends. She might forget people's names but never their family situations now, envying them the simplicity of lives untouched by tragedy. Their not being haunted by a moment they would give anything to relive.

Jen collected her papers and packed them in her briefcase. When she turned around, she saw Chuck Woodley, her superior, sitting in the back of the courtroom. He rose when she approached him.

"Checking up on me, Chuck?"

He shot her a disappointed stare. "If I thought that was necessary, you'd be on suspension now. I've got some news."

He moved further in along the bench and Jen took a seat next to him. Woodley wore dark suits that always looked wrinkled. He had come to the district attorney's office out of law school and had never left, trading security for ambition. His stomach had begun to sag over his belt and his light hair never seemed to vary in length or style. Around them, the courtroom continued to empty, a few looking briefly their way before filing out.

Woodley leaned toward her on the bench. "The Feds say if you wear a wire, they can make everything go away."

"A wire?"

"You know the drill. Show up and get the transaction on tape. Then testify at the arraignment."

"They agreed to this?"

"They suggested it. I guess it comes down to priorities, and nailing this dealer is a hell of a lot more important to them than nailing you. Lucky thing."

"For who?"

"This is a no-brainer, Jen, an absolute no-brainer."

"Not from where I'm sitting."

Woodley stiffened and his face got a little red, darkest where his hairline had begun to recede. "Let me give it to you from where *I'm* sitting. You've got a chance to walk away from this. Turn their offer down and the only place you'll walk is jail."

Jen suppressed a shudder. "Last week, I was only trying to save my career. What happened?"

"Things changed."

"Like what, Chuck? Trying to grease a little butt on your own? Land one of those cushy federal prosecutor jobs if you deliver me on a platter?"

Woodley's expression didn't waver. "I'll keep you out of jail, Jen. That's the best I can do."

"What if it's not good enough?"

"Then you've got a problem."

Jen stood up and clutched her briefcase. "I'll let you know, Chuck."

"Don't take too long."

CHAPTER TEN

Over the next month, Jamie settled into a pleasant and easy routine. Two full weekends of clinic sessions had acquainted him with the various procedures and disability specific training methods. Simply put, everyone could ski if they wanted to and were willing to give the instructors a chance to teach them.

As a junior instructor, Jamie began as a spotter and backup, often doing little more than lending moral support. By Christmas vacation, though, he had progressed to the point where Marge was giving him his own students to solo on the many weekdays when he was available. Patience was crucial and, much to his own surprise, he found he had plenty of it, stemming from the fact that he was at least as grateful to be at Loon Mountain as his students were.

He got a job at a nearby inn doing whatever was needed. Front desk on some days, waiting tables or maintenance on others. The modest hours left him plenty of weekday time to spend at the school, the relative quiet of the mountain doing wonders for his training process and allowing him to take on more responsibility with students.

Finding a place to live proved even easier. Gus and Jed rented a townhouse in Alpine Village, located barely a mile from Woodstock Station off Route 3. Since they made their home solely on the first floor, the second was uninhabited, giving Jamie two bedrooms and one bath to himself. And sharing the rent three ways made for a payment he could easily afford.

It was a place to live, but not a home really, at least not in the sense Jamie had known in Rhode Island. That and Meg were the only things he still missed, the two being intertwined in random thoughts that came at night sometimes.

The house he had sold to Mrs. Dellagash was an old, rundown Victorian that had long ago been chopped into three apartments, one per floor. The original owners had built it in the 1850s as a home for slaves who had made their way to freedom, a fact duly noted on a plaque mounted on the front porch to commemorate its historical status. He and Meg had spent every spare hour for months patching and painting, repairing what they could and replacing what they couldn't. They would work long into the night and then sleep on a mattress in the middle apartment they had decided to keep for themselves.

It had taken all of a spring, summer, and fall to finish, the work completed just before the first snow. To celebrate, Jamie and Meg drank champagne amid sawdust, stepladders, and paint cans. They had saved their apartment for last to renovate, and the fact that it was their own home made the work a delight every step of the way. Meg bought all of the furniture, a piece at a time mostly, Jamie rushing home from work every day just to see what about the apartment was different.

That first summer the house's electrical system was too burdened to add air conditioners to its load. But he hadn't minded it at all, especially on nights when it was too hot to sleep and they'd lie next to each other atop the bedsheets. Close enough to feel the heat rising off her skin, shuddering as he drew a line of sweat with a finger down the center of her spine.

Always practical, she had warned him the house was too expensive, but Jamie had insisted they'd get by. And they would have if the family business—and his job—hadn't died with his father a year before. Meg had already gone back to school and Jamie wanted to let her stay there, waiting to tell her until it was too late in the semester to get the tuition refund that would have helped them make it. He talked Meg out of taking a leave to get a job, insisting he could find a decent one himself.

He tried putting a résumé together for the first time and tore it up after each effort. Going into his father's business had always been the plan, his death as impossible to foresee as the business's virtually immediate downfall without him. Jamie had gotten through college without giving much thought to his future and, as a result, had never really planned for it. He tried more menial, minimum wage jobs, but none of them lasted, and when they did, not a single one provided enough to even meet the expenses of a house he really couldn't afford to begin with.

Jamie had known Meg was getting fed up, could feel it in the cold shoulder she turned to him at night, stiffening under his touch. He thought it would pass. They'd get by because they always had. They'd even survived the strain of going to different colleges a thousand miles apart. Get through that, Jamie always figured, and they could get through anything.

What's changed? he had asked her one night.

Nothing, she had replied coldly. *That's the problem.*

A few days later he had come home and found her note.

Even up here in Loon the loneliness on the bad nights ate away at him, keeping him vaguely in touch with that part of himself that had sought death in a bathtub and then fled north when the effort failed. But the long days on the slopes filled his life with purpose and challenges that made his own pale by comparison. Especially on weekends, when you could barely move in the controlled clutter of teachers and students squeezed in the school's small headquarters. People always coming and going, leaving their problems somewhere else. The triumphs of his students became his own triumph, and there were far more than he could claim personally, at least in recent memory. The days left him with a sense of accomplishment, which the nights could whittle away at but not erase. And most days his efforts left him so exhausted he was able to fall into a deep sleep. Jamie was building something here every bit as real as the house he and Meg had repainted, rewired, and rebuilt; it just hadn't taken its final form yet.

Then, on a weekday just before Christmas vacation, he had found himself working with a woman in her thirties named Sheila Stone, who'd broken her neck on a high dive into a swimming pool. She'd regained feeling in her hands and arms, but remained paralyzed below the waist. She was a regular at Loon and had gotten quite good on a bi-ski.

On her sixth run, Jamie watched Sheila working the outriggers determinedly to direct her bi-ski down the slope. He had helped her settle into it hours before, working the strap around her waist and threading it through the safety latch.

"Is that too tight?" he had asked.

"I wish I could tell you," Sheila grinned.

It was one of the mistakes that was all too easy to make: forgetting that some skiers about to spend a good part of the day on the mountain had no feeling in their lower body. Jamie had learned to just grin back instead of apologizing in embarrassment.

It had been a mistake not to break for lunch, but the crowds had thinned somewhat and Sheila had squeezed in a second extra run as a result. Still, she seemed to be wavering a bit now, looking suddenly fatigued. Jamie could see her hands shaking on the outriggers and her eyes beginning to flutter an instant before she swerved off the slope not far from the bottom.

Jamie reached her as something like an electric shock

tipped the bi-ski over and left Sheila writhing madly in the snow, in the throes of some kind of seizure. Jamie undid the strap and hoisted her spasming form gently out of the bi-ski. Then he laid her down on top of the snow, feeling the slight bulge just below her waist.

Oh no . . .

It was a catheter, and with a cold smack to his stomach Jamie realized that he had forgotten to ask Sheila if she was using one. He had made the restraining strap too tight as a result. The subsequent pinching off of her urine flow had brought on a kind of toxic shock. Gus Bocamper happened to be working the same intermediate trail and skied over, instantly recognizing the symptoms.

Ski patrol personnel arrived on the scene less than two minutes after Gus had summoned them on his walkie-talkie. Sheila's spasms slowed, then stilled, as they treated her. Her vitals were stable, but she was unconscious and the ski patrol opted for the safe strategy of transporting her by the mountain's ambulance to the nearest hospital.

"What should I do?" Jamie asked Gus, as soon as the ambulance left.

"Tell Midge before someone else does."

"Looks like somebody else already has," Jamie said, watching Marge striding purposely toward him.

"It's called autonomic disreflexia," Marge told him on the way back to the school headquarters. "It's also called screwing up. You should take a look at our questionnaire sometime."

"We got a late start."

"You never asked her if she was catheterized, did you?"

"No."

"What were you thinking?"

"I wasn't."

Marge shook her head. "I guess not. When it comes to yourself, that's called bad judgment. When it effects someone else, it's called irresponsibility, and up here that gets people hurt. People like Sheila come to the mountain to forget about why they need a bi-ski or a catheter. They depend on us to make that happen for them and when somebody screws up, we fail."

"I understand," Jamie said.

"Do you?"

"I think I came up here to forget something too."

"And I gave you a chance."

"I know."

"What I'm asking is that you give your students that same chance. If you can't do that, you haven't learned anything and your stay on this mountain will be a short one, I shit you not."

"Sheila?" Jamie asked hesitantly.

"She's going to be fine. Might even be skiing again to-morrow."

"With me?"

Marge narrowed her gaze. "Nope. You've earned your-self another assignment."

"His name's Bobby Cohen," Marge said when they were back inside the school, as she handed Jamie a file folder. "Twelve years old and severely autistic. We call him Snowman. Loves it up here. Parents say he's never happier."

"So what's the problem?"

"You'll see."

CHAPTER ELEVEN

"Notice anything?" Marge asked, after Jamie had read Bobby Cohen's history the next morning.

"No catheter."

"Anything else he hasn't got?"

Jamie scanned the file again, afraid he'd missed something. "No."

"How about a skiing history?"

"He's been coming for two years."

"But he's never skied. Not even a foot. We've tried everything. Most instructors consider it a victory if the boy just keeps his skis on. Oh, one thing I forgot to ask: do you like movies, hotshot?"

"Why?"

Marge just smiled.

Bobby Cohen arrived at the entrance to the school a few minutes later. A bit small for his age but other than that, he looked no different than any other twelve-year-old boy. Refusing to let the boy's past daunt him, Jamie introduced himself to Bobby and shook his hand.

The boy looked up with his unchanging expression and said, "Bond. James Bond."

Jamie went through his introductory words enthusiastically, pausing at all the right moments so Bobby could comment. But the boy never said a word, just kept staring straight ahead, more through Jamie than at him, expression utterly blank. Jamie asked another instructor to stay with the boy for a few moments. Then he ducked back inside Marge's office.

"You forget to tell me something?"

"You forget to get the complete history again?"

"The kid doesn't talk, does he?"

"He talks just fine."

"But he doesn't ski."

"Not yet."

"Well, he's going to ski today."

Outside he helped Bobby into his right ski. When he started on the left one, the boy popped his foot out of the right.

"Difficult to ski without that," Jamie said.

"What will I do?" Bobby asked him. "Where will I go?"

It took some coaxing, but he managed to get the boy over to the beginner area. Getting him to leave his skis on was another matter entirely. An hour into the morning they were no further along than Bobby had ever gotten before.

"I'm not going to give up like the others," Jamie told him finally. "You and I aren't leaving this mountain until you ski."

"I think this is the beginning of a beautiful friendship," the boy told him in his droll monotone.

And then Jamie realized what the other instructors must have already known: Bobby's sole means of communication was reciting lines from films. That, coupled with his affinity for the mountain, had led to him being nicknamed "Snowman" in reference to the Dustin Hoffman character in the film *Rainman*.

This time Jamie kept talking while he refitted the boy's skis. "How'd you get that?" he asked, pointing to a small bruise on the boy's cheek.

"This was no boating accident," Bobby said back.

"It was a shark," Jamie followed dramatically.

Bobby's lips quivered, flirting with a smile. "I'll catch this bird for ya, but it's not gonna be easy."

"Robert Shaw," Jamie chimed in. "Try this one," he added, readying his best Brando. " 'Charlie, I coulda been somebody. I coulda been a contenduh.' "

"Marlon Brando," Bobby said, a little louder than before. But there was an air of condescension in his voice, as if the line had been too easy.

Bobby's skis were fastened on tightly by then and for the first time he didn't try working them free.

" 'I like my nose, Mr. Cross. I like breathing through it,' " Bobby droned nasally, altering his voice.

"Jack Nicholson, *Chinatown.*"

Feeding him another line back, Jamie fastened a ski bra to the tips of Bobby's skis and wrapped a tether around the boy's waist. Before Bobby knew it, Jamie had aimed him sideways away from the base lodge and pushed. Suddenly the boy was skiing, held to Jamie by the tether the whole time.

A few minutes, and lines, later Jamie had gotten Bobby up the slight hill between the double chairlift and the base lodge. Controlling him with the tether, he actually had Bobby skiing, at least wedging with the help of the ski bra.

A few short runs later, Jamie held his breath and released the tether. Much to his delight, Bobby held his own, needing only Jamie's hand on his jacket to glide to a stop. Once, when Jamie failed to latch on quick enough, Bobby fell but barely missed a beat as Jamie hoisted him back to his feet. The boy moved steadiest when it was his turn to quote, eager to see if Jamie could get the answer right, seeming utterly oblivious to the skis on his feet.

Jamie initially kept his quotes to popular films, but he soon realized he didn't have to; the kid was a walking cinematic encyclopedia, apparently having memorized every movie he had ever seen, which might well have been every movie ever made.

In which case why wasn't Bobby trying harder to . . .

"You little bastard," Jamie said under his breath, because the kid was keeping the game simple for *him*. Knew all along he could stump Jamie anytime he desired, but wanted to keep the game going as badly as Jamie did.

And that meant, maybe, he wanted to ski.

Jamie gradually increased the pace as Bobby got the hang of balancing himself. Eventually the boy stopped looking at him and began to focus on the trail ahead, gliding over the snow he had only looked at in the two years of visits up until today. The lag between movie quotes grew longer, as did the unbroken stretches they covered.

By midafternoon, Jamie had progressed to the lower points of Sarsaparilla. He was tempted to let Bobby try it with poles in hand, but decided to put that off for another day, wary of exhausting his supply of movie quotes.

That evening, at the instructors' daily wrap-up meeting, he received a standing ovation for his efforts and a gift Marge herself had rushed into town to fetch:

A season's pass at the Lincoln Four Cinemas.

CHAPTER TWELVE

"So you haven't made up your mind yet?" Dr. Ryerson asked, facing Jen from her chair.

"They've given me until next week. After that, I guess I can consider myself fired."

"Have you talked to Matt about this?"

"He's got enough problems without worrying about me."

"So you're saying it doesn't work both ways."

"I caused his problems." Jen hesitated. "What do you think I should do?"

"Are you asking me about Matt or Woodley's offer?"

"Woodley's offer."

"You wouldn't still be putting the decision off, if you didn't have serious problems with it."

"There's a big downside, but you'd think I'd be used to downsides by now." Jen stopped, but Dr. Ryerson urged her on with her eyes. "Until the accident, I thought I was ready to make the move to a downtown firm. It's all I thought about." She sighed. "I don't think I've thought about it at all since. I miss that. I miss being able to focus on something that's within my power to achieve."

"You don't think it's within your power anymore?"

"I don't know. Maybe it is; I mean, it could be. But it's not within my power to help my mother or Matt."

"Which makes you feel worse?"

"I owe it to Matt to be able to do more for him. Did I tell you what it was like when he was fitted for his first prosthesis?"

"No," said Dr. Ryerson.

"We went to this office where the limbs, arms and legs, were on display everywhere. We were discussing options and timetables, and all I could think about was this was all my fault. We were there because of me. The best I could do for my brother was tell him which leg looked best on him."

Dr. Ryerson made some notes on her pad.

"The technician got one of the prostheses strapped on, and it felt so good to see Matt standing again; I mean, from the waist up, you'd never even know anything was wrong. I looked at him and thought maybe there's a way out of this, after all. Maybe we could get things back to where they were.

"Then he fell.

"He wasn't supposed to walk yet, but he took one step and went down. I went down with him inside, because I felt bad for me, like I had lost another chance. The technician took lots of measurements and explained the whole process. It's amazing what they can do with prosthetics these days, truly amazing."

"I know," said Dr. Ryerson.

"The technician explained that because he still has his knee, Matt will barely even limp eventually. And, with further advancements in prosthetics, he might even be able to run a marathon some day."

"Impressive."

"But after hearing all that the only thing I could think of when we got home was watching him fall."

"Did he get up?"

Jen narrowed her gaze." Of course."

"How?"

"Reached out and grabbed a chair, I think."

"The technician didn't help."

"Maybe a little."

Dr. Ryerson made some more notes.

"Why is that important?"

"Because you said he fell; you didn't say he got up."

"Like the glass being half empty or half full?"

"Something like that, yes."

Jen's mind was back in the prosthetics office, thinking about what had happened next. "The technician told us the goal of prosthetics was to provide a totally normal life, that Matt would be able to do ninety to ninety-five percent of everything he'd done before. I sat there nodding, even though I knew the ten or five percent that prosthetics couldn't bring back was everything to him. It was gone because of me, and I've got to find a way to give at least some of it back to him. Because if I don't, all I'm ever going to see is him falling, not getting up."

"Are you trying to save him?"

"Yes."

"Why?"

"I just told you that."

"Why?" Dr. Ryerson repeated.

"Why don't you tell *me* for a change?"

"All right."

Ryerson flipped to a clean sheet of paper and jotted down a name and an address.

"What's this?" Jen asked, after the psychiatrist had handed it to her.

"You want to see Matt get up instead of fall. This is how."

CHAPTER THIRTEEN

Jamie shifted agilely on the slope behind the bi-ski that was slicing down a trail called Bear Claw before him. Since the Sheila Stone incident, Marge hadn't let him solo with any skier he could take out of her sight. She called it indefinite probation on some days, infinite probation on others. Jamie didn't argue.

"You're doing great, Kendra," he heard Frank Rawley say in a gravelly voice in front of him. "Absolutely fantastic."

Three years earlier a bad fall off a horse had cost fifteen-year-old Kendra the use of her arms and legs. She could use her hands a little and twist her head from side to side, enough to let her fully enjoy the ride down Loon Mountain. The bi-ski in which Jamie and Frank had placed her at the top of the trail had a seat bucket with suspension mounted on two radically side-cut skis and fixed outriggers on the sides. Jamie rode shotgun in the rear, while Frank had tether lines looped tightly on his wrist connected to the back of the bi-ski with a carabiner.

Before him Jamie could hear Kendra squealing with delight the faster Frank let her go. He was letting her whiz down the Bear Claw at a moderate clip, but that was still slow by the standards Jamie used to ski by.

Until that day on the Chute eight years ago, speed had been everything. Now it held no meaning. Jamie was content to let the world slip leisurely past him. After three months up here, he had never once skied all out and had no urge to do so. It was a test he had no need to take, much less fail. His leg had cooperated thus far, providing the excuse he needed to leave the black diamonds to others.

Suddenly Jamie saw Frank Rawley stumble on his skis. Frank tried to right himself, failed, and flopped hard into the snow.

That's when Jamie noticed that the tether in his hand had torn loose from the carabiner, leaving Kendra to barrel down Bear Claw with no means to stop herself. Her bi-ski cascaded over a slight drop and picked up speed rapidly, heading straight for the Mountain Club hotel, which lay across a thin walkway a hundred yards down.

Jamie kicked hard and followed Kendra, letting go, climbing to full speed for the first time since the accident. He felt nothing but the familiar spray of the wind in his face, sharp needles alive against his skin. Kendra's bi-ski was flying, but in no time Jamie was flying faster. He weaved through the jagged line of shocked skiers, watching others dart for dear life from the bi-ski's path, as it sped to within fifty yards of the hotel.

Jamie banked to the outside as if he were racing it. He drew even, then surged ahead to gain the angle he needed to close the gap. He was near enough to the hotel to see the mountain reflected in the nearest windows when, still picking up speed, he twisted both ski tips to the left and cut sideways across the powder. He nearly lost his balance, but shifted his weight at the last instant to keep from tumbling.

The final seconds came in a flurry of white kicked up around him. As the bi-ski approached, Jamie had just enough time to turn his skis right toward it and dive. His upper body hit the front tip, turning the bi-ski sideways and away from the Mountain Club. The bi-ski whistled briefly against the packed powder beneath it before finally grinding to a halt.

Jamie watched from the snow, laying there as he had after popping a ski on the Chute eight years before, afraid to move for fear of what he might feel. Tentatively, he propped himself up to a sitting position before the first bystanders reached him. He shifted slightly and nothing scary begged him to stop. He noticed a patch of blood forming beneath his left leg, but the gash, suffered in the collision with the bi-ski, wasn't deep.

He turned around to face the bi-ski and saw Frank Rawley already tending to a shaken Kendra. Jamie staggered to his feet and moved toward them, favoring his bad leg. But it was only a little sore, and putting pressure on it reminded him that he had just skied all out for the first time since the accident that had nearly crippled him.

"Good thing you're not hurt," Marge greeted Jamie when she arrived, brushing past him to check on Kendra. "We can't afford to be a man down February school vacation week."

CHAPTER FOURTEEN

By the time Jamie arrived at Woodstock Station that night, the gang was into their second pitcher of beer. Gus and Jed were both there, the fronts of their wheelchairs wedged against the square table. Brad Weatherby, a college student with the worst fake ID Jamie had ever seen, was sitting with them, nervously as always, certain he was going to get caught. Brad was seated next to Beth Langhorn, a graduate student at Dartmouth who was part Navajo.

"Now hold on a minute," drawled Gus when he saw Jamie approaching. "Look who we got here. It's Crash Brooks. Give us the instant replay, Jed."

Needing no further prodding, Jed grasped a pair of glasses and turned them into skiers plowing down a beer slick table. He made a whistling noise and imitated the path Jamie had used earlier in the day to bring Kendra's bi-ski to a halt before it crashed into the Mountain Club.

"Boom!" he said, and at impact both glasses shattered.

"Slow motion, cuz, let's see it again!" urged Gus.

"Stop," pleaded Brad Weatherby." Everyone's watching us."

"Wondering when you're gonna start shaving probably," quipped Gus. "What are ya, boy, sixteen or seventeen?"

"Shut up."

"You was smart, son," Gus continued, "you'd ask Merlin to make you an ID that actually worked."

"Never saw him make anything that didn't," Jed affirmed. "Old guy used to be an engineer is what I heard."

"No," said Gus. "Retired janitor—that's what somebody told me."

"Sanitary engineer, then."

"Hey, Beth," Gus said and then looked back at Jamie, "what's the Navajo word for crash?"

"Ahscrewme. We need more glasses," she added and rose to get them.

"Pull up a chair, cuz," greeted Gus. "I'd offer you mine, but then I'd be on the floor." Gus drained the rest of his beer in a single gulp. "What'll you have? The choices are several. The pitcher on the left or the pitcher on the right."

Beth Langhorn returned and plunked a glass down before him.

"Surprise me." And Gus took a pitcher in either hand and filled Jamie's glass with equal amounts from both. "Can I ask you guys something?" Jamie asked, after taking his first sip.

"Finish your beer first, cuz," Gus said, tipping his mug.

Jamie took another sip. "What's Marge do in the real world?"

"This is her world," Jed answered.

"I heard she was born on the mountain," Gus added, pouring himself another glass.

"She's got a family of her own," said Beth Langhorn. "For eight months of the year anyway."

Jed nodded, his lips full of suds. "I met them last year. She was one of the founding fathers—"

"Mothers, cuz," Gus corrected.

"Okay, *mothers* of adaptive skiing. We're going back twenty years now, to Winterpark."

"She showed up wanting to ski," Beth picked up, "and they didn't have any equipment for her."

"Makes you wonder where we'd all be," Gus reflected, "if she'd just climbed back in her car and drove off."

Jed raised his mug. "I for one would be better off for never meeting any of you assholes. A toast to—"

"Hold on," Gus interrupted. "Check out the bar. Third stool from the end."

Jamie turned in that direction and saw a woman seated there nursing a cigarette and a mixed drink.

"Guys, do we have to do this tonight?" Brad Weatherby asked nervously.

"What's the matter?" asked Jed.

"Afraid she'll recognize you from homeroom, son?" Gus asked.

"It's the rule," Jed reminded them. "Anyone we see alone we invite to join us."

"So why is it always women?" Beth challenged.

"To achieve a balance, in case you hadn't noticed."

" 'Course, girl," said Gus, "if you want to be the one to invite her over . . ." And he flapped his eyebrows dramatically

"After spending all this time with you guys," Beth chided, "don't think I'm not tempted."

Gus leaned forward in his wheelchair. "Hey, Beth, what's the Navajo word for lesbian?"

"Better-off."

"Okay," said Jed, "closest to the glass."

He centered his empty in the middle of the table while the others pulled pennies from their pockets and flung them into the air with a flick of a finger. A chorus of metallic pinging sounds followed as the pennies rained back down to the table. Gus's glanced off the rim of the empty glass.

Jamie's landed square in the suds.

"I should get another shot, being disabled," Gus protested.

Jamie stood up and tapped the side of Gus's wheelchair. "No drinking and driving allowed in the bar anyway."

The closer he got to the woman, the more attractive she became. She wasn't quite beautiful—more self-assured, with strong features that couldn't quite mask the loneliness reflected in a distant gaze Jamie had come to know all too well. Her face was framed by the furls of cigarette smoke floating through the half-light. They trapped her features in a shroud of shadows, like a character from an old Bogart movie. Ida Lupino, or Lauren Bacall, maybe Ingrid Bergman with an attitude. Will, the bartender with the duckbill baseball cap and biceps Jamie had met that first night he'd driven north, had just set a fresh drink down before her when Jamie got there.

"Hi," he greeted, "a few of us noticed you were alone. If you want some company . . ."

She made no move, displayed not a flicker of change in her expression. "No thanks." Barely audible.

Jamie should have left then, but he couldn't take his eyes off her. She had hair the color of chestnuts and even smoking looked good on her.

"Waiting for somebody?" he tried.

"Nope."

"How about if I sit down here?"

"Be my guest." She swung a little toward him as he took the stool next to her, just in time to catch the smoke she blew in his face.

"I should take that as a hint, right?"

"Now you're getting the picture."

"You always act this way when people are trying to be nice?"

"Is that what you call it?"

"Just my nature."

She turned back to her drink. "Well, take your nature and sit down somewhere else."

But Jamie still couldn't leave.

"Do you ski?" he asked her, grasping now.

"No."

"What brings you to Loon?"

"Overpriced bars where I can meet people I don't want to talk to."

Jamie might still have persisted if he hadn't caught the start of some commotion out of the corner of his eye. He slid off the stool and returned to his table to find Gus Bocamper glaring up into the eyes of a tall, lanky college-age kid. The kid had drawn the chair they were saving for Frank Rawley away from the table.

"I'm telling you," Gus told him, like he'd said it before, "the chair's taken."

"I don't see anyone in it now," the college kid said, a little drunkenly.

"He's coming, boy. Let's leave it at that."

The kid tensed. "Did you just call me 'boy'?"

"Would you prefer asshole?"

The college students at the next table stood up en masse.

"Excuse me if I don't join you *boys*," Gus spat at them.

"Tell you what," the lanky kid sneered. "Just give us *your* chair."

Gus didn't miss a beat. "Deal," he said, pushing himself down out of it, settling onto his stumps and shoving the wheelchair backward against the kid forcefully enough to make him wince.

It was hard to figure what was going to happen next; the lanky kid glaring down, Gus glaring up atop his stumps, and Jed grabbing a beer bottle off the table by its neck.

Then Frank Rawley appeared at the front edge of the

crowd that had formed around the fracas. Jamie had never seen Frank actually smile, but he was coming as close as he ever did now. His facial muscles twitched, his arms like coiled springs dangling by his side.

"Anybody save me a chair?"

Jamie couldn't tell who the question was aimed at, but the college kids at the next table sat down again, leaving the tall, lanky one to face Frank alone.

"Right here, bro," Gus called from the floor, dragging the empty chair out from under their table. "Guess you won't be needing this, boy," he said to the tall kid. Then he pushed off with his stout arms and swung himself agilely back into his wheelchair.

"Thanks," Frank told Gus, sliding into the chair saved for him without taking his eyes off the students. The rest of them rose together and huddled briefly with the tall, lanky one before swaggering toward the door.

Jed poured Frank a beer and slid it over to him. Frank took the glass in hand without ever moving his gaze from the retreating college kids. Even after they left, his face kept twitching. He drained the beer as if it were water.

"We're gonna be seeing them again," Rawley said softly.

CHAPTER FIFTEEN

The adaptive ski school was overbooked as always during February school vacation, and Marge was juggling instructors and schedules even as Tuesday morning's students began to arrive.

"You ready to solo again, Brooks?" she asked Jamie, standing behind the counter next to the school's computer.

"My indefinite probation over?"

"Indefinitely."

"In that case, I can't wait."

"It's a first-timer."

"All the better."

"Let's hope so," Marge said, handing him a file folder and highlighting the details in staccato fashion. "Last-minute addition, a favor for an old friend. Single amputee. Fifteen-year-old boy. Three months since the accident. Details inside. Waiting right over there by the door. Go introduce yourself."

Jamie checked the folder and then moved toward the entrance to the school headquarters. The boy was leaning against the wall near a table, trying to put his weight on a prosthetic leg he didn't quite trust yet.

"Hi, Matt, I'm Jamie Brooks."

He extended his hand and Matt reached out to take it. Their eyes met and Jamie was struck by the feeling that he knew this kid, that they had met before. Something about his deep-set eyes, the color of his shaggy hair . . .

"Do I know you?" he asked lamely.

"You know me," a voice said from the doorway.

Jamie turned and saw the fading smoke first, drifting in a cloud through the door from the hallway beyond. The young woman who entered holding the cigarette wore tight jeans and a ski jacket that fit the lines of her body like a glove. Her face was rigidly set, her expression fixed as it had been when Jamie took the stool next to her in Woodstock Station the night before.

"I'm Jen," she said. "Your student's sister."

"There's no smoking in here."

She looked at the dying butt in her hand. "Consider it my disability."

"You told me last night you don't ski."

"That's right. But my brother does." Jen sucked in her lips. "Maybe you should get started with him before the snow melts."

THREE

CHAPTER SIXTEEN

Matt knew Jamie was looking at his leg, figured maybe he should just yank up his ski pants and show him the titanium prosthesis he had from the knee down. Maybe tell Jamie the thing hurt like a bastard, and explain how the doctors called it phantom pain but couldn't explain why it went away when Matt rubbed the shaft of the prosthesis, which looked like a shock absorber for a car.

As a kid he had always wanted to be an X-Man, have steel instead of skin so bullets would bounce off him. Well, he had steel now but there weren't any bullets, and nobody had told him steel hurts just as bad.

People kept telling him he had lots to be thankful for, though it seldom seemed that way. Sure, only three months after waking up to find his leg looking awfully short beneath the hospital bed sheet, he was able to walk with barely any limp at all on his prosthesis. But walking was the only thing he *could* do.

In the hospital, when he had first looked at the missing piece below his knee, Matt wasn't scared because he could feel the rest of his leg down there. Fiery hot and throbbing like somebody had wrapped it too tight with athletic tape. He couldn't say when the reality dawned on him; he remembered trying to cry out only to find himself caught between breaths. He thought he was gagging and then a nurse was at his side slipping a needle into his arm. Matt dreamed that night about cutting 720s and doing rails on his skates. Shredding his jeans on the pavement, the hems dragged low, bleeding threads.

Matt couldn't remember the accident itself, only staring straight ahead to see the red light an instant before the Jeep flew through it. The rest didn't exist, a big swatch sliced from the fabric of time.

New time started up again when they strapped on his first prosthethic leg, fresh from the limb factory. The therapists got him walking, even though it felt as if somebody had stuck a pogo stick under his knee. Matt held on to the parallel bars a little less every day as he walked, until he could manage it with arms swaying almost normally by his sides. With jeans on, hanging low over his sneakers, it was hard to even tell anything was wrong.

Then he had gone back to school, everybody looking at him while pretending not to. They either stared or turned away, nothing else, and none of them knew what to say because there was really nothing they could say. Every minute was torture, as Matt saw hard and fast all the things he'd never be able to do again. His best friends, meanwhile, were always busy with something else—those things, mostly.

He had already asked the therapist about playing soccer again, and his new leg started to hurt as he listened to the honest response. Matt bent over and pretended to adjust the prosthesis the way they showed him. But what he was really doing was rubbing it like skin and bone, making the pain go away.

Matt left the hospital on two crutches, which later became one. Then there was the cane. He hardly used it at all anymore, walking just fine without it. But everytime he crossed the invisible line that put too much stress on his steel leg he felt it buckle, letting go, the titanium a part of him strictly on its own terms.

At night sometimes, when his leg itched with phantom pain, he strapped the prosthesis on and rubbed it in search of relief. His brain didn't seem to know the real leg wasn't there anymore, allowing him to fool it by scratching the fake one.

But he couldn't trick it into letting him kick a soccer ball. He was just standing around in the high school gym, where he hung out any time he didn't have to be anywhere special and sometimes even when he did, when a ball squirmed its way out of a mesh bag and rolled straight for him. Matt planted his weight on his prosthesis and tapped the ball forward, holding his breath. Then he retrieved the ball and reversed his feet, planting his weight on his real foot and kicking out with the steel cant wedged into his matching sneaker.

The ball rolled across the shiny gym floor, bouncing off the bleachers, but Matt didn't note the moment of impact. He hadn't even realized he had struck the ball until it skittered in front of him.

Strangely, that simple moment more than any other showed him that everything he had based his life around was over. All the determination and rehab in the world weren't going to make steel feel like skin and bone. He could live with the falls and the fittings, because they were getting him somewhere, were something he had to go through. But the truth was they'd never get him where he wanted, and had always expected, to go.

Matt slammed his steel foot into the ball again, and this time it veered clumsily sideways, coming to rest against a wall, where he left it. There would be no more dribbling through sliding tackles to make the perfect cross the way he used to. No more launching the ball like a rocket and hearing the hard wisp when it lodged home in the net.

No more lots of things, because his brain could get things down to his knee, but after that it was anyone's guess what happened next. So what if he was getting real good at walking again, if that was all he'd ever be able to do?

"Let's sit down over here," Jamie said to him, pointing to a table. "The faster we get this done, the faster we can get started."

CHAPTER SEVENTEEN

"I've got a questionnaire here we need to fill out."

Jamie led Matt to a table, but the boy showed no interest in sitting down. Instead, Matt flipped through the pages of the questionnaire, frowning.

"This supposed to help me learn how to ski again?"

"You already know how to ski."

"I'm talking about beyond the bunny trails."

"So am I. In fact, I'm talking about skiing as well as you did before, every place you skied before."

Matt let the questionnaire flop to the table and shrugged. "Yeah, right."

The kid reminded Jamie a little of himself at that age. Hair long and mussed. Eyes more questioning than trustful. Every motion punctuated with a shrug.

"What level skier are you?" Jamie asked him.

"You mean, was I."

"No, that's not what I mean."

Matt looked down, then up again. "I was pretty good."

"Diamonds?"

"Yeah."

"Want to ski them again?"

The kid frowned. "Sure. As soon as my leg grows back."

"Why wait?"

"I gave up skiing anyway. Decided to concentrate on soccer."

"You good at that too?"

"I was. Junior national team."

"Pretty impressive," said Jamie.

"Think you can get me to play soccer like I used to, too?"

"One sport at a time," Jamie said, as Marge moved up alongside him.

"Why don't I handle the questionnaire?" she said, half winking. "Just to be on the safe side."

"What did she mean by being on the safe side?" Jen asked when she and Jamie were standing alone in the lodge hallway.

"Your brother doesn't have a catheter, does he?"

"No."

"Then don't worry about it."

Jen looked at him questioningly. "I guess I owe you an apology. For last night."

Jamie shrugged her off. "No need."

"Yes, there is: I should have offered you a cigarette. I thought that's why you didn't come back."

"So now you find out I'm going to be your brother's instructor."

She met his stare. "I was hoping for someone with more experience."

"Marge has her reasons."

"She says she's got a feeling you and my brother might hit it off."

"And you don't agree."

"I heard what you said to him," Jen said, brushing the hair from her face. "About skiing as well as he did before, on the same trails, too."

"So?"

"Did you mean it?"

"It's what this program is all about."

"Save the sales pitch."

"You wouldn't be here if you hadn't heard it already."

Jen felt for her cigarettes. "Can you smoke in here?"

"No."

"Let's go outside."

"Can't smoke there, either."

"Forget it. I can wait."

"To blow smoke in my face again?"

"You like how that feels?"

"Not particularly."

"Because that's what my brother's felt like since he realized soccer wasn't going to happen for him again anymore. What he said about the junior national team was true. He would have made it next year, as a sophomore. One of the top twenty players in the country." Jen felt for her cigarettes again. "So a therapist I've been seeing recommended this place as an alternative."

"I thought we were talking about Matt."

"Dr. Ryerson, the therapist, skis; I don't."

"I could teach you."

Jen smirked. "I don't fit the profile."

"There isn't one. Three months here, I've learned that much."

"He passed," Marge said, handing the questionnaire back to Jamie. "Just one more thing to do before I hand Matt over to you."

Marge fished from her pocket a metal ball, like a fishing sinker, attached to a string.

"Ever seen one of these before?" she asked, flashing it before Jamie and Jen. They both shook their heads. "It's called a plumb bob. Used mostly when hanging wallpaper to make sure it's straight, or by carpenters in their work."

Marge bent down gingerly on her small legs and balanced the ball so it fell between Matt's big and second toe through his ski boot.

"What I'm doing here is checking the body's center of mass, taking a measurement to make sure we get the ski flat. Now there's plenty of high-tech gizmos for doing this, but the plumb bob works just fine in my book." She looked up at Matt. "I think we've got a ski here that'll do the trick." Marge repocketed the plumb bob and gazed back at Jamie. "What do you say we go get him rigged?"

Back on the equipment aisle, Marge selected a ski and handed it back to Jamie. Then she plopped a pair of outriggers into his arms.

"Wouldn't this kid be better off with somebody who has more experience teaching three-tracking?" he wondered.

"Don't think you're up to the task, hotshot?"

"I haven't soloed with a three-tracker yet, that's all."

"Sometimes there's more important things than experience. Matt's angry." Marge smirked a little. "Reminds me a little of you three months ago. You know I never asked what brought you up here. Never asked Cap either."

"I'll tell you if you want."

"No need. Whatever it was, you walk through that door and you leave it behind you, just like our students do. They walk through the door and you see some accident of birth or bad fortune. Either way, the physical wounds are long healed by the time we get our first look. What hasn't healed is what's going on inside, and that's why this program is as popular and successful as it is." Marge turned around and faced Jamie. "We can't give that boy out there back his leg. But we can give him back part of what the accident took away."

Jamie laid the equipment atop a table and flipped open the yellow folder containing Matt's file.

"Looking for something?" Marge asked him.

"How he lost his leg."

"Car accident."

Jamie looked up from the folder.

"The rest isn't relevant to what he's doing at Loon." Marge stopped. "No more than how you hurt your leg is."

"Cap didn't tell you?"

"He tried to. I stopped listening when he mentioned a certain trail we don't talk about here anymore. With a student, sometimes it's better to let him tell it on his own, should he choose to. You knowing more than he's ready to say himself isn't always a good thing."

Jamie nodded and gathered up the equipment again.

"What do you think of his sister?" Marge asked suddenly.

"I think anger runs in this family."

Marge nodded. "Now you know everything that matters. The whole relevant history."

"I miss something here?" Jamie asked her.

"Not yet."

CHAPTER EIGHTEEN

"Three-tracking," Matt repeated, after Jamie had explained the process to him. They were outside on the patch of snow just beyond the base lodge, which was perfect for getting new students started.

"You've skied on one ski before, right?"

"Plenty of times, but not with, what do you call those things?"

"Outriggers."

"I'd rather use poles."

"These will be easier for you to handle, give you a bigger margin for error."

"Then things aren't gonna be the way they used to, are they?"

"We've got to start somewhere."

Matt glanced down at his prosthesis. "Why can't I just leave this thing on and ski with two skis?"

"Because your stump can't take the weight yet," Jamie said, laying the ski down next to Matt's remaining foot. "You've got to wait until the healing process is complete, so you don't screw up the fit and maybe do permanent damage."

"I'd say the damage already done is pretty permanent."

Jamie stood up and handed Matt the outriggers to balance himself. Then he helped the boy remove his prosthesis and leaned it against the wooden rack behind them.

"What happens if we come back and it's gone?"

"We look for someone with three legs," said Jamie. "Now try putting your weight on the outriggers. Like they're crutches. Get the feel of them."

Matt managed that much with no difficulty.

"Next," Jamie continued, "pull on the cords to bring the flip-skis up and make the tails—"

"Claws."

"Okay, *claws* dig into the snow. This is the position you want to use when you're going to push on flats."

Matt did as he was told, then worked the cords up and down a few times to get used to the feel. "Do I really have to use these?" he frowned. "Can't I just use poles?"

"Eventually. I told you, these are better for starters."

"I'm not a beginner; you said that yourself."

"The outriggers will let you progress faster at three-tracking. But first you've got to get used to them."

"How?"

"Let's get your ski on first."

He picked up the ski Marge had chosen and positioned it alongside Matt's boot. Matt balanced himself on the outriggers, handles looped through his gloves, as he eased his boot into place and locked in the ski.

"Keep the weight on the outriggers and lift your ski in the air," Jamie said, demonstrating the motion with the single ski he was wearing and the outriggers he had equipped himself with. "Now turn the ski to the right, then the left. Work on getting the feel."

"Balance drills," Matt said.

"Right."

Matt lowered his ski back to the snow. "Okay. What's next?"

"Walk on them, first with the flip-skis up. Push off on the claws and slide the ski."

Jamie watched Matt struggle at first with the awkward motion. But he quickly found a smooth rhythm.

"Now try it with flip-skis down," Jamie said from behind Matt, showing him how to push on the inside edge of both outriggers simultaneously. "Now hop!"

Matt was quick to grasp this movement too. When he seemed comfortable, Jamie added a slight rotary motion to the outriggers, and Matt handled the drill nicely.

"Good," Jamie said. "Now put the flip-skis down and let's just walk a little. Push on the inside edge of both outriggers and slide the ski."

"I know what to do," Matt said.

But he was wrong, and Jamie elected to let him slip off kilter a little and find his own way back.

"How good are *you*?" Matt asked, as he eased himself determinedly along.

"Not much at all anymore."

"What about when you were?"

"Champion in the under-eighteens."

"When?"

"Eight years ago."

"What happened?"

"I quit."

"Why?"

"I got hurt."

"Broke your leg, something like that?"

"Something like that, yes."

Matt stopped, breathing hard. Jamie noticed he had drawn his flip-skis up, the routine almost natural already. "You quit because of a little old broken leg?"

Jamie pulled his ski pants up so Matt could see the scars. "Compound multiple fracture and a torn patella tendon. Not much left whole between the knee and the foot. They saved the leg. I was lucky."

"I wasn't."

They worked the slight trail back and forth almost to the chairlift to give Matt a feel for using the outriggers with his remaining leg.

"I think we're ready for a trail now," Jamie said, sensing Matt's impatience. "Let's move over here to Kissin Cousins."

"Some trail," Matt snickered.

"Wait until you've fallen a few times."

"What makes you think I'm going to fall?"

"Because I'm going to teach you how to get up and I don't want my time wasted."

They skied the short distance to the beginner trail together, Jamie still on one ski.

"They tell you how I lost my leg?" Matt asked him.

"A car accident, that's all."

"My sister was driving. You like her?"

"I think so, yeah."

"She hasn't got a boyfriend. Nobody serious for awhile."

"Good news."

"No, it's not; there's a reason why."

"What is it?"

"She doesn't want one. Like she's punishing herself."

"Because of the accident?"

"She was punishing herself even before," Matt said, and left it at that. "How much you know about our situation?"

"I didn't know you had a situation."

"Better that way."

"Whatever you say."

Matt ground his flip-skis home again. "So teach me how to fall."

Within an hour, Matt was following Jamie down Kissin Cousins, matching his gliding motions perfectly. Jamie gradually increased the pace and sharpness of the turns along the slight grade. Matt fell a few times and had trouble getting up at first until Jamie's words finally hit home.

Make sure your stump is positioned uphill. . . .

Put the outriggers flip-skis down in claw position. . . .

Put the downhill rigger across your body close to the shoulder, uphill hand flat on the snow and push up, swinging the rigger to the downhill side. . . .

Drag it up with you as you bring your body back over the ski. . . .

But he didn't trust having only one ski under him yet. Just like he didn't trust kicking a soccer ball with his prosthesis, or walking in the hall between classes when everyone in the world was watching him.

After they reached the bottom after a sixth run, Jamie skied on and Matt pushed off to catch up.

"Hey, where you going?"

"Chairlift to try a different trail, called Snubber. Wanna come?"

Jamie showed Matt how to align himself in front of the chair using his outriggers for balance so the tram would scoop him up.

"I thought it'd be harder," Matt said, once they were seated on the lift.

"Give me time. I'll find something difficult for you."

As they rode the chair up, Matt looked toward the south

side of the mountain, then back at Jamie. "Ever hear of the Chute?"

Jamie felt something flutter in his stomach. "Uh-uh."

"Yes, you have. Everybody who skis New Hampshire has."

"It doesn't exist. Just a story, a legend."

"I know people who've skied it."

"They tell you that?"

Matt's expression wavered. "They told other people."

"They lied."

Matt gazed toward south mountain again. "It's out there somewhere, isn't it?"

"No," said Jamie, as their car squeaked along.

CHAPTER NINETEEN

Jamie was waiting when Jen came into Woodstock Station that night, seated on the same stool he had occupied briefly the night before.

"This taken?" she asked, indicating the stool next to his.

Jamie pulled the stool away from the bar. "Been saving it for you."

Jen sat down and drew an ashtray toward her. Same one, Jamie thought, he had used to burn Mrs. Dellagash's eviction notice three months before. He had spoken to his former landlord twice since then on the phone, promising to make good on the back rent and making arrangements for what little remained in his apartment to be placed in storage. There wasn't much more in his life he needed to put in order, and what there was he'd get to a little at a time. Up here, time didn't mean as much, and what there was seemed to form its own reality.

Jen lit a cigarette, ordered a vodka tonic.

"Matt did great today," Jamie said, sipping his draft.

"He doesn't think so."

"First day, for Christ's sake."

"He's had a lot of first days these past three months. The second tends to be not much better."

The bartender set Jen's drink down before her. It had barely hit the napkin when she lifted it up and began sipping through the straw.

"We covered three trails," Jamie told her.

"Beginner level," she said.

"Tomorrow we'll move on to intermediate."

"And by the end of the week . . ."

"What do you want me to say?"

"That by the end of the week he'll know he'll be able to do something with one leg as good as he used to with two."

Jamie pulled back a little, twirled the beer glass in his hand. "It's only February. The season still has some time left in it."

Jen was slurping her drink now, the straw making a fizzing sound against the naked ice cubes. "That's if I can get him to come back," she said, and took another long drag on her cigarette.

Jamie leaned over and took one from the pack, putting all his weight on his bad leg. The pain dug in and held, feeling like glass slivers poking at his flesh from the inside.

"You all right?" Jen asked him.

"I'll be fine," he said, grimacing. "It's just my leg. Old accident. It's okay unless I overdo it." Jamie winced again.

"Anyway," Jen said, "I thought you didn't smoke."

"Only when I drink."

"Bad habit."

"Smoking or drinking?"

"Take your pick."

Jamie looked at her as he lit his cigarette, let it dangle at arm's length after a single puff. "I have."

"If I can't get Matt to come back, who else you gonna bum cigarettes off of?"

"Guess I'll have to find someone else to blow smoke in my face."

"I've prosecuted people for less than that."

"Then I should file charges."

"Try sexual harassment."

"Ah, the catch phrase of the nineties."

"It gets plea-bargained down to misdemeanor malicious mischief. I get six months suspended."

"Off the hook until you blow smoke into the next guy's face."

"Maybe I'm already on probation."

Jamie finished his beer. "I didn't know you were a lawyer."

"And I still have no idea what you are."

"Yes, you do."

Jen went to work on her second drink; the straw bent inward she was sucking up the vodka so hard. "Did Matt tell you anything about how he lost his leg?"

"Car accident. You were driving."

"What else did he say?"

"That's all."

"He left something out."

Matt thrashed about in bed. He'd given up trying to sleep an hour before and switched on the television. Flipped through the channels long enough to be sure there was nothing he wanted to watch. The picture glowed off the wall, the sound a dull hum in the background. There was a movie on with a bar scene, and that reminded Matt of the night before the accident.

"Welcome to The Underground. Four dollars, please."

Matt fished the singles from his pocket and handed them to Calvin, the club owner. This being all-ages night, Calvin hadn't asked to see his ID. But at The Underground they didn't ask to see ID no matter what ages-night it was.

The hard riffs of rock music that had been muffled in the parking lot pained his ears as he stepped inside.

The floor felt sticky and the aroma of stale beer hung in the air along with the cigarette smoke that formed a cloud near the ceiling.

Matt headed left toward the bar and pool tables, where the smoke hung just as heavy, but the blisteringly loud music coming from the stage was easier to take. A crack that sounded like a gunshot sent pool balls scurrying across the well worn green felt, and Matt followed Walker Long sinking balls, cigarette hanging from his mouth. Waited until the game was over to make his approach.

"I think you've got something for me."

Walker took Matt gently by the jacket and led him to the bathroom. Inside there was a padlocked door that somebody had kicked in. They went into that stall.

"You play soccer," Walker Long said suddenly.

"Yeah."

"I used to play soccer."

"I know," Matt said and pulled a wad of cash from his pocket.

"I found the pills in his jeans the day of the accident," Jen finished.

"So you lost it. You snapped at him. Perfectly understandable."

"It happened in the car. We were arguing."

"You caught your brother using drugs. What were you supposed to do?"

"You don't get it, do you?" A look between anger and pain squeezed Jen's face taut. "Matt wasn't the one using; I was."

CHAPTER TWENTY

"He bought them at the bar, before I had a chance to that night. He must have overheard me making the arrangements. That's what we were arguing about in the Jeep." Jen's voice grew pained. She snubbed out her cigarette but stopped short of reaching for another. "That's why I didn't see the light change."

Jamie sat there. For an instant he had to remind himself to breathe. He didn't speak because he couldn't, all words stuck deep in his throat.

"I caused the accident. Matt lost his leg because of me. . . . Well, aren't you going to say something?"

"Not about this."

"Am I making you nervous?"

"No."

"Surprised that I'm such a loser?"

Jamie caught his breath, and his words, again. "That's not what I was thinking."

"Wait. There's more: One of the guys working with this drug dealer was a federal agent. The Feds had a pretty good case built up against the dealer and guess who's name came up in the course of the investigation?"

"Matt's?"

"And mine. But the Feds were most understanding. They

told my boss I could keep my job if I wore a wire. Nail the dealer cold."

"And you said . . ."

"I was supposed to give my boss an answer today. I came up here instead."

"Loon has telephones."

"I'll keep that in mind."

"And there are also other times you could have come up."

"None better than February school vacation."

"You ever hear of weekends?" Jamie asked her.

"I needed to come up now. And I know what you're thinking."

"You were wrong before."

"You're thinking I should be ashamed of myself. That I've got no business taking care of a kid if I can't take care of myself."

"Wrong again. Sounds more like that's what *you're* thinking."

Jen stared vacantly at the bar. "Things got to be too much. I started losing hours. Or the ones I had weren't long enough."

"So you started taking speed . . ."

She frowned, lowered her gaze further. "Breakfast of champions, James."

"Matt found out."

"Kid got what he wanted, though," Jen said ironically. Her expression sagged. "I haven't taken anything since the accident. Flushed the pills I had left down the toilet."

"What you pulled out of his jeans, you mean."

"Yes, as a matter of fact." Jen sucked the glass up to her face. Jamie watched the liquor dodge past the ice cubes. "It feels great to be clean, let me tell you."

Jamie hesitated. "You telling me this because you want something?"

"Yes. Concentrate on getting Matt to ski again. Don't worry about me."

He shook his head. "Sorry. I help Matt, I help you. One way or another."

"I don't ski. I told you that."

Jen started to raise her drink again, but Jamie clamped a hand onto her wrist and stopped the glass where it was.

"How about I teach you?"

She looked at him incredulously. "Maybe tomorrow."

"What's wrong with now?"

"Now?"

"I'm sure we can find some skis that fit you."

"But it's, it's . . . dark."

"A common occurrence at night."

"You said your leg was sore."

Jamie took the glass from her hand, the cubes jiggling against each other. "I'll ice it later."

They drove to the mountain in separate cars and parked near the Governor Adams Base Lodge, on the other side of the trail line from Loon's Mountain Club hotel where Jen and Matt were staying.

"You never answered my question," she said to Jamie, as he worked his keys around, trying to find the one that opened the main door.

"Which one?"

"What you do with your life."

"Lately I've been starting a new one."

"Sounds like a good idea."

"It was sort of forced on me."

"What happened?"

Jamie tried another key. "Lots of things. None of them good."

"I can recommend a good pusher."

"I got my stuff legally."

"The truth comes out . . ."

Jamie flashed a look that made Jen feel like someone had slipped snow down her shirt. "We both were trying to do the same thing. I just tried to do it faster."

Jen swallowed hard. "You going to tell me what happened?"

"Take a guess."

"Your girlfriend left you."

"Walked out and took most of the furniture."

"Why would she do a thing like that?"

"Her note said things weren't working out."

Jen smirked. "That's what we always say, James."

Jamie let the keys dangle. "But I'd never heard it before. Meg was the only serious girlfriend I ever had. Since tenth grade. I knew we'd always be together, that things would always be the same."

"What changed?"

"Nothing—that was the problem—especially me. Here I was, twenty-four years old, still thinking the same way I did when I was in high school. I always knew what I was going to do and it all fell into place. Meg, a job with my father's company, a house . . ."

"Something must have fallen out of place."

"My father died. The business collapsed. I lost my house. And by the time I looked in the mirror and found I wasn't seventeen anymore, I found Meg's note, too."

"So how did you end up here?"

"I skidded off the road."

"The truth, please."

"That is the truth, actually. I ended up in the place where I could go back to being seventeen again and nobody would notice."

"But you became an adaptive ski instructor instead."

"They had an opening."

Jamie went back to his keys and finally found the right one. A single light was on inside the lodge, enough to illuminate a path to the adaptive ski school headquarters.

"What else?" Jen persisted, following close behind him.

"Keep your voice down."

"We're the only ones in here."

"We won't be if you don't keep—"

Jamie froze. Before him, the entrance to the school's headquarters had been shattered around the latch.

"Oh, shit," he muttered.

Jen came up alongside him and grasped his arm, as Jamie shoved the door open wide.

FOUR

CHAPTER TWENTY-ONE

"All right," Marge said to the group squeezed around a pair of tables in the adaptive ski school headquarters early the next morning, "it's business as usual today. We're going to do our jobs and let the Lincoln police do theirs."

Jamie heard a few of his fellow instructors snicker at that, and Marge didn't bother to reprimand them.

"I know what's on your minds," she continued. "But we got people counting on us today, and those people are a lot more important to me—and to you—than what happened here last night. Anybody got a problem with that?"

Apparently, nobody did.

Marge surveyed the room, nodding. "Okay. I'm sorry to have interrupted your morning runs. Let's get to work." A flurry of activity amid the requisite muttering followed, briefly broken by Marge. "Except Jamie, Frank, and Gus. My office. Now."

The night before, the Lincoln police had arrived shortly after Loon's own security force to find much of the adaptive equipment in the front room smashed and broken. The pictures that had adorned the walls lay in heaps of broken glass on the floor; they were crunched and shattered into smaller bits beneath the feet of the first few officers to enter. Stepping on Hope Mountain's history. Stepping on dreams.

Jamie's dismay turned to outrage when he saw the mono-ski mangled on the floor. The white message board had been torn from the wall and left atop it, a message hastily scrawled in red marker:

THANKS FOR THE CHAIR

"I get the feeling you know who did this," Marge said accusingly, her office door closed for the first time Jamie could remember. She spoke to all three of them, but her eyes were fixed mostly on Frank Rawley.

Rawley's face twitched, first the left side, then the right.

"Frank?" Marge prodded. "There something you want to say?"

Rawley's face twitched again, just on the left this time.

Marge stepped out from behind her desk and stopped in front of Gus Bocamper's wheelchair. "What about you, Gus? Anything you want to tell me? Something that happened a couple nights ago, at Woodstock Station maybe?"

Gus looked at Jamie and then at Frank. "Well, sheee-it. I swear the woman's got cameras everywhere in town. . . ."

"You know who did this or not?"

"We know," said Jamie, leaving it at that.

It seemed like a long time before Marge spoke again. "Okay, now listen close. I'm going to give it to the three of you from the book. This stopped being our problem when the Lincoln police got involved. Everything you do, whatever it is and wherever you do it, reflects on this program. And the donors who help support us wouldn't take too kindly to three instructors ending up in jail. Equipment is a lot easier to fix than reputations, boys, I shit you not."

Marge stopped and leaned back against her desk. Something in her face changed. Jamie had seen that look before, when he had forgotten to ask about Sheila Stone's catheter and a crisis was barely avoided. But this look was scarier and he could have sworn he saw Marge's face twitch a little like Frank Rawley's.

"Like I said," she continued, "that's from the book. Now that we've got that over with, you're gonna hear it from me." She leaned forward and fixed her stare on all of them at once. "Kick their ass."

CHAPTER TWENTY-TWO

"Let's start with a review of what we did yesterday."

Matt plopped his weight on his outriggers and shrugged. "We didn't do anything worth reviewing yesterday."

"You mind letting me be the judge of that?"

"So long as you tell me what's the use."

"You want to ski. . . ."

"My sister wants me to ski."

"You want to ski diamonds. Just give me a chance."

"I'll give you until Sunday," Matt said.

"You want to be skiing diamonds again by Sunday?"

Matt nodded dramatically. "You're right. That's not good enough."

"Meaning what exactly?"

"I'll show you later."

"What's wrong with now?"

"You said you wanted to review."

With that, Matt mounted the chairlift effortlessly and they headed up to a beginner trail for one run before moving on to intermediate. Jamie knew a three-tracker could ski any trail with no limitations. Eventually, with a "ski leg," Matt could go back to regular skiing, again without limitations. Even a standard prosthesis, like the one he had now, could be used with modifications as simple as pulling a tight elastic sleeve up over the knee and thigh to stabilize the stump pistoning and rotation. But that was out of the question for Matt until at least next season, which left this one strictly for three-tracking.

Jamie started with a review of the traversing procedure to develop lateral movement.

"As you cross the slope—"

"Remember to hold the outriggers shoulder width apart and keep my body flexed," Matt completed with a sigh.

Jamie skied up alongside him. "Let's try it together."

Together they cut across the fall line of the slope, Matt not missing a beat.

"How do you stop?" Jamie quizzed.

"This some kind of quiz?"

"Just answer the question."

"Claw of the outriggers by turning across the fall line."

"Do it."

Matt turned the tips of his outriggers up and dug the tails into the snow, hop-turning back around to face Jamie as he came to a halt.

"I'm impressed," Jamie told him. "See, you can forget all the fancy terminology. In the end it all comes down to instinct, but in your case that instinct has to be reeducated. What is skiing about more than anything else?"

"Balance."

"And everything we're working on, all these exercises and drills, are meant to develop that sense of balance on one leg, not two. How far did we get into garlands yesterday?"

"Not very, because you talked too much."

"You remember what garlands are for?"

Matt rolled his eyes. "To work the beginning and end phase of a turn."

"So what we're going to do now is start steering the foot

into the hill." Jamie demonstrated. "By applying pressure to either the big or little toe depending on which way you want to go. See?"

"You're steering."

"Now you try."

It took a few minutes of wavering and slipping, but Matt quickly nailed the maneuver. The same held true when they moved on to uphill christies to get Matt used to performing controlled skids to regulate his speed and stopping motion into turns.

"Use your knee," Jamie called, as Matt skied by. "Slow down into the turns, but accelerate as you come out of them. That's it."

Finally Matt turned his ski fast and sent a shower of snow spraying back into Jamie, who smiled.

"I think we're almost ready to have some real fun."

"Why do I have to take my ski off?" Matt protested, after they had skied down to a flat spot at the bottom of the trail. "You call this real fun."

"I said almost. Now take it off."

Matt popped his boot free of the binding.

"Okay. Balance yourself on your outriggers like this," Jamie said, imitating the motion with his poles. "Then twist your boot from side to side, flexing it up and down."

Matt tried, didn't look happy about it. "Why are we doing this?"

"Because to steer, you want to use the foot in a rotary motion like the one you're practicing now."

That got Matt working harder.

"Get back into your ski," Jamie said after nodding his satisfaction.

"Finally . . ."

"Not quite."

"Now what?"

"You ready for advanced parallel turns yet?"

"With these?" Matt shot back, holding up his outriggers.

Jamie smiled, came up just short of mentioning how deftly and naturally Matt had balanced himself on one leg. "Good point," he said. "For advanced parallel turns, you've got to use them like poles. Now, what I want you to do is touch one outrigger, flip-ski down, lightly on the snow while you lift the other outrigger into the air. Other side now. Keep repeating the motion. . . . Feel how your body arcs naturally toward the side of the down outrigger?"

"Just like with poles," Matt realized.

"Exactly. Let's try it in motion."

That meant another trip in the chairlift, Matt antsy during the ride up. Jamie kept the pace slow on the way down and Matt took the trail gracefully, falling only twice as he practiced the more advanced method of turning down the slope. He didn't seem to fear falling nearly as much as yesterday, although he remained self-conscious about the stares some of the passing skiers cast his way.

"Be nice if we could go somewhere nobody got in our way," he said when he reached the bottom just behind Jamie.

"Tough to find a place like that on a school vacation week."

"Not really," Matt said." I went for a walk last night and found one."

Matt led the way through the woods to the south, following a different path on his ski than he had taken on foot last night along South Mountain Road when he couldn't sleep.

It had been cold outside, but the wind had died down for the night, making it actually feel warmer than it had during the day. Matt let himself walk aimlessly along the road until he came to the foot of a trail that appeared out of nowhere. The world, shrunken in scale, narrowed into a roadbed of twisting white above him.

"This is the Chute, isn't it?" Matt asked, after their hike had taken them to the top rather than the foot of the slope.

Jamie didn't answer him, remembering the last time he had stood in this spot. The Chute started out at a moderate grade but narrow width, with a dangerous tree line on the right and a rock bed on the left. From this vantage point, the start alone was visible. But Jamie remembered how the Chute widened to a sheer grade that steepened between the trees and rocks all the way to the bottom. It wasn't scary until after the first bend had passed and the bulk of the slithery trail came into view.

"Knock, knock," Matt pestered. "Anybody home?"

"It's the Chute, yes," Jamie conceded, feeling like he had a stomach full of snow.

"You said it didn't exist."

"Wishful thinking on my part."

"Forget diamonds," Matt told him. "This is the trail I want to ski."

"You see those signs we passed back there?"

"What signs?"

"The U.S. Forest Service signs that said no trespassing."

Matt smirked. "They gonna shoot us?"

"Take a turn on the Chute and they won't have to."

Jamie thought back to his accident again, his mind freezing on the moment Cap Morgan had found him half buried in the snow.

But how had Cap beaten the rescue team here?

"We've got four more days," Matt said before Jamie could

consider the question further. "I want to ski this before I leave on Sunday."

"Pick another trail."

Jamie thought Matt was about to get angry. But his face went eerily calm instead. "I'm getting sick of people telling me to pick something else. I'm talking about people like you and my sister. You tell me to do this and that, and when I try you say, 'Wait a minute, it might be too hard. Try this instead.' "

"Sometimes we're right."

"Right about what? I can't do anything the same as I used to, *nothing!* Come on, name something I can. Try!"

Jamie just looked at him.

"So you know what?" Matt continued. "This time I'm not going to bother trying to do something I could do before; I'm going to try something new. I'm going to try the Chute, no matter what you or anyone else says."

"You won't be the first to regret it," Jamie said, leaving it there.

"Some things you've got to experience for yourself."

"Not this."

CHAPTER TWENTY-THREE

Jamie found Marge on the Picaroon. He stopped to the side of the trail and watched as she seemed to push a young girl up the mountain a shove at a time. One strong thrust after another from the front, the young girl learning to find her balance better each time. Bending at the knees and leaning forward, no longer wavering when Marge shoved upward on her shoulders.

The girl was a four-tracker: two skis and a pair of outriggers that matched Matt's. From this distance, Jamie couldn't tell what her disability was.

Marge caught sight of him as she skied back down the trail just behind the young girl. Gave her some words of encouragement and then skied over to Jamie.

"Her name's Beckie. I've been working with her, well, forever—seven years anyway. She has spina bifida. Makes walking hell. First day out here she skied between my legs, me holding onto her the whole time." Marge looked over toward Beckie as the little girl carved her way adroitly down the trail. "Now she wants to be the first four-tracker ever on the woman's disabled ski team. So go figure."

"I've got a problem with Matt, Midge."

"Eighty percent of all problems here are equipment related. They can be fixed. Talk to Merlin."

"Matt wants to ski the Chute."

"Never heard of it."

"Unfortunately, Matt has."

Marge chuckled. "Looks like I was right on the money when I paired the two of you together. Knew it as soon as I laid eyes on him, all you had in common."

"I've still got two legs."

She shook her head. "I'm not talking about legs, hotshot, I'm talking about *eyes*. I look into the kid's eyes when he first walks into the office and I see yours three months ago when you first got here. Two of a kind, let me tell you."

"The Chute, Midge."

"You'll talk him out of it."

Jamie hesitated. "I'm not really sure I should."

Marge narrowed her gaze at him. "So which punishment are you ignoring, the five thousand dollar fine or year in jail?"

"Neither."

"Then why are we having this conversation?"

"I think I've got a way around this. But it's important that Matt believe we're gonna let him do it."

"We?"

"Right."

"But we're not going to let him ski the Chute."

"We're not; we're only going to make him think we are."

Marge chuckled. "You are a genuine piece of work, hotshot, let me tell you."

"Will you go along with me on this?"

Marge looked undecided. Then their eyes held and her expression softened.

"Your eyes," she said. "They look a lot different than they did when you got here. I go along with this, you think Matt's eyes will look that way when he goes home?"

"That's my hope."

"Be easier if I just fired you."

"That's the truth."

"Goes against my instincts, though. Aw, to hell with it. If you think it'll help this kid, I'll tell him the goddamn Easter Bunny just did a triple flip three-sixty turn on Big Dipper."

CHAPTER TWENTY-FOUR

"What are we doing here?" Matt asked that afternoon, after Jamie had led him into the well-stocked, mirrored gym in the Mountain Club where Matt and Jen were staying at the foot of the mountain.

"I've only got until Sunday to get you ready to ski the Chute. That calls for extraordinary measures. First thing you need to do is take off your prosthesis."

"Why?"

"Because you don't use it when you ski." Jamie zipped open his gym bag. "In here. C'mon, let's go."

Matt unstrapped his leg and let Jamie stuff it into the bag, accepting a pair of outriggers in its place.

"No snow in here I can see," Matt noted.

"Use your imagination."

"I'd rather use skis on the slopes."

"First we need to do some things that can't be done on the slopes. To three-track a trail like the Chute you have to have the same sense of balance with one leg that you used to have with two."

Jamie reached into his bag and came out with an eighteen-inch-long board. He turned it upside down to show Matt there was a baseball attached, a bolt drilled straight through its center thanks to Merlin.

"You get your sports confused?" Matt joked.

"Watch," Jamie said, as he lay the board on the gym floor. It flopped slightly to one side until Jamie stood atop it, his feet straddling the position of the baseball. The board jerked a few times but then settled into an even keel. Jamie looked like a surfer, shifting his weight slightly and continuously to keep it off the ground equally on both sides. Balancing himself to cut out the wobble.

"The baseball's like the trail and the board's like your ski," he explained, holding his balance easily now.

"I'm supposed to do that with one leg?"

"That's how you ski, isn't it?" Jamie stepped off the board, grabbed Matt's outriggers off the floor, and handed them to him. "Try it with these first."

Matt climbed on and the board flapped beneath him, even when he used the outriggers for balance. Finally he got it stable, his foot directly over the baseball.

"Okay," Jamie said after he'd been standing that way for thirty seconds.

Matt let the board flop to the right, thankful to take the pressure off his leg.

"Now I want you to do the same thing again, only this time as soon as you're balanced, flex your outriggers under your arms. Like you're racing downhill."

Matt tried it a few times. He could get one outrigger up but the second always left him tilting. Finally he lowered both outriggers and left them on the floor.

"Why'd you stop?"

"Because I suck."

"And you'll suck on the Chute too, unless you keep trying."

Matt gritted his teeth and tried again.

"You're trying to balance yourself with your arms," Jamie advised. "But what's holding you back is your leg. You've got to bend it more. Put more weight over the board, just like it's a ski. Try to imagine you're soaring down the slope."

It took a few attempts until Matt finally managed to keep the board from swaying; at first just briefly, but then a little longer each time. He held the outriggers behind him, tucked low, imagining himself soaring down the Chute.

They moved on to the weights next, where Jamie let Matt strap on his leg again.

"Leg press machine first," Jamie said, after leading him to it.

He showed Matt how to lie down with his back pressed into a hard pad, his good leg extended almost straight in the air against the rubber guide attached to the weight rack. Then Jamie slapped a twenty-five-pound plate on either side of the sled.

"What's skiing have to do with lifting weights?"

"In your case," Jamie said, "it's not lifting weight, it's *balancing* weight. Turn those handles toward you to release the sled. . . . Now, ease it down, bending at the knee. Then lift the weight back up again."

Matt repeated the motion fifteen times until Jamie told him to stop. Then he angled Matt's foot to the inside on the rubber rest of the sled.

"When you shift your body skiing," Jamie explained, "different parts of your thigh absorb the weight, which means each of those parts has to be capable of balancing it. Release the sled."

After another fifteen reps, Jamie angled Matt's foot so the toes were pointing to the outside.

"Go," he instructed.

They repeated the sequence of different angles three more times, Matt's thigh starting to really burn by the end.

"Okay," Jamie said, leaving him no time to rest, "next exercise."

They moved to the leg-extension station at the Universal machine, where at least Matt could sit up straight. Jamie stuck the pin at seventy pounds. Matt's ankle was curled under a softer, round pad this time. Jamie had him raise his good leg up, keeping his toes pointing straight up, until the leg was fully extended, the pad parallel to the floor instead of perpendicular to it.

They finished the set, and Jamie instantly slapped the pin into the next hole up the stack.

"Go!" he said.

After ten reps, he raised the pin again.

"Go!"

Another two sets later, Jamie positioned Matt's foot under the pad so his toes were pointing in. Fifteen reps later, he pointed the toes out. And when that was over, he helped Matt down and led him to a Smith machine: a floating bar rigged into a cam that could be set at any level for safety. Jamie wrapped a pad around the bar and adjusted it to be level with Matt's shoulders.

"Squats now."

Jamie helped Matt angle himself so his shoulders were under the bar and his leg centered beneath him.

"No weight?" he asked.

"Not the first set. I just want you to get the feel of the motion."

Jamie got him stable and then slipped on a few plates. Held his shoulders again, then slowly eased off so Matt was balancing the bar on his own. The weight wasn't heavy, but with only a single leg to support him the squatting motion proved very difficult.

Matt was sweating by the end of the exercise, sick of looking at himself in the mirrors. He wanted to sit down, settled for leaning against the wall.

Jamie squirted some water from a plastic bottle into his mouth and then handed the bottle to Matt.

"One more thing and then we can go back to the slopes," he said and dragged a flat bench to him. "You're going to jump up on the bench and then jump back down. Keep going until I say stop."

Matt looked at him incredulously. "After all those sets, you want me to do *this?*"

"What do you think your leg's going to feel like near the bottom of the Chute? You've got to learn to keep going, no matter what."

Matt started jumping. Without Jamie having to tell him, he flexed his knee as he landed on the flat bench, absorbing the weight to keep himself balanced. After a few initial stumbles, he got the hang of it and settled into an easy rhythm. Jumping back down was harder but he soon smoothed that out too.

"For the next three days," Jamie said when Matt finally sat down, exhausted, "you're going to repeat these exercises in the morning, and then again in the afternoon."

Matt looked up at him strangely. "The Chute's where you hurt your leg, isn't it?"

"Yes," Jamie managed, taken aback.

"Ever try skiing it again?"

"No. Once was enough."

CHAPTER TWENTY-FIVE

"Some of the lights are on," said Jed. "They could be home."

"Why not ski up to the front door and ring the bell?" Frank Rawley asked, shaking his head as he set a trio of fire extinguishers down in the snow at the edge of the clearing.

Beyond Frank and the others lay a sprawling expanse of condominiums and houses that dotted the eastern side of the mountain in the Beachwood development, but they were focusing on one duplex in particular. Gus Bocamper had asked around Woodstock Station and found that the college kids they had confronted Monday night, the ones who vandalized the ski school, were staying in the right half of that duplex.

Gus looked back at Beth Langhorn. "Hey, Beth, why don't you check for a fresh trail or something?"

"What?"

"I thought Injuns are supposed to be able to do that. At least offer some words of wisdom."

Beth rolled her eyes. "They're not here. But they will be back before we're finished, if we don't get moving. How's that?"

Frank Rawley turned to Jamie. "James." He never said much; he didn't have to make his point.

Jamie started forward when Gus's voice froze him. "Wait a minute, why do you guys get to do everything?"

"Because we can reach the doorknobs," Frank told him.

"Ain't you ever heard of the Americans with Disabilities Act?"

"How does it apply here?"

"Equal opportunity to mess people up. Equal opportunity to extract some sweet revenge. Equal opportunity to have a shit-kicker of a time." Gus's face got a little serious then. "And that mono-ski these boys busted up used to be mine."

Jamie and Frank looked at each other. Rawley's face twitched a bit as he nodded. Then he took the two containers of Superglue from his pocket and handed one each to Gus and Jed.

"I'll take the back door," said Jed.

"I guess that means I'll take the front," added Gus.

Without needing to be asked, Frank went with Jed and Jamie with Gus. Beth Langhorn played lookout, as Jamie followed Gus away from the tree line. Both Gus and Jed were on mono-skis. Not the best way to make a surreptitious approach to the condominium, but under the circumstances the best available.

There were three steps leading up to the condo's front door, and that's where Gus parked his mono-ski. He hopped out onto his stumps and looked up at Jamie.

"This is where I'm gonna need your help, cuz."

Jamie squatted and looped an arm around Gus's shoulder. Gus cupped his opposite hand around the lower part of the railing, pulling as Jamie helped hoist him up the steps.

He was breathing hard when Jamie deposited him at the front door. Gus smiled as he drew the tube of Superglue from his pocket and unscrewed the cap, then raised the tip of the tube up toward the lock centered in the doorknob.

Even though Jamie could see Gus straining to reach it, he left the task to him, stealing a few glances back at Beth in case she spotted anyone coming up the road. Gus had to push up off his stumps, but he managed to slide the tip of the tube into the hole and squeezed until the glue started to collect outside it, the lock gummed up good.

"How long?" Gus asked.

"Frank said five minutes before it hardens."

"Shee-it, sounds like my pecker."

"Took you long enough," Jed said from the bottom of the stairs as Gus finished, Frank Rawley scouting the area with his eyes.

"I don't recall no steps at the back door for you to climb up, cuz," Gus snapped and eased himself back down the stairs alone, careful of the ice and snow.

They gathered again at the edge of the woods to wait.

Twenty minutes later, they were still waiting.

"Cold as a witch's tit," Gus said, bouncing around on his mono-ski to stay warm.

"Just the way we want it," Jed added.

They all turned when headlights poured up the road. Frank Rawley was the first to recognize the Ford Explorer. Jamie noticed his face twitching a little more than usual. Frank reached down and grabbed one of the fire extinguishers, sliding the other through the snow toward Jamie. Beth Langhorn knelt and got the third one ready.

The Explorer pulled up in front of the condo. The lights and engine sounds died. Then the doors clanked open, allowing the five college students Jamie remembered from Woodstock Station to pile drunkenly out and lurch up the walk. Jamie watched one of them fumble for his keys and then jam one toward the lock.

He knew the plan had succeeded when the kid kept working it around, trying unsuccessfully to jam it in.

"Lemme try," another of the college kids said, pushing his way forward.

"Go to hell."

"You bent it, goddammit!"

"Gaw head and try yours, then."

"I'm going around the back," said the tall, lanky one with blond hair who had started things off three nights back.

Frank Rawley glanced over at Jamie. He didn't speak, but his eyes said, *Get ready.*

The five kids met up again halfway between the Explorer and the front door, kicking at the snow and swearing up a storm.

"Let's go," Frank Rawley said, and Jamie moved with him out of the darkness.

They had the fire extinguisher hoses raised and ready well before they drew within range.

"Hey!" was all one of their targets had time to shout before Frank and Jamie charged the last stretch of the way and opened up with their extinguishers.

The water sprayed the college kids in a frosty mist that turned almost instantly to ice. Frank and Jamie had drenched them thoroughly before they realized what was happening. And by then the water soaking through their clothes, and freezing over their hair and faces, left them too numb to retaliate.

When they tried to move, Beth Langhorn swooped out, barely disturbing the snow as she rushed the Explorer, and emptied her extinguisher into the doors to freeze the jambs and locks up tight as well. By the time all three charged back to the tree line, weapons abandoned behind them, Gus and Jed had already skied back toward the center of the mountain, their hoots and hollers echoing in the night air.

The college students chased them, but quickly gave up the pursuit in favor of finding a way to de-ice themselves. Hardly an easy proposition when the doors to their condo were Superglued closed and the doors to their car frozen shut. They'd probably break a window eventually, but that would take time, leaving them even more frigid and uncomfortable. Cold air flooding the condo all night long.

Just what they deserved.

Many of the other instructors were waiting back at Gus's and Jed's condo in Alpine Village to celebrate the anticipated victory. The triumphant cries that spilled from Jamie's car as they pulled up in front of the door gave the report better than any words to those eagerly assembled within.

Jamie couldn't remember a time he had felt better, so much a part of something. He felt no guilt whatsoever over what they had done; the college students had this coming to them and even more. If they were smart, they would leave things as they were. Jamie didn't want to think about what Frank Rawley would do to them next if they didn't back off.

He was making his way through the back-slaps and handshakes of the crowd gathered inside, accepting a chilled bottle of beer when he saw Gus waving the cordless phone at him.

"Phone call, cuz!"

Gus tossed the phone to him and Jamie caught it in his free hand." Hello."

"It's Will," said the bartender from Woodstock Station. "Can you get down here?"

"Why?"

"Just make it fast."

CHAPTER TWENTY-SIX

"How long ago did she leave?" Jamie asked.

"Couldn't be more than a few minutes," Will said, between drink orders. "I tried to keep my eye on her, but it's a busy night."

Jamie stiffened. "You didn't let her drive?"

Will frowned and flashed a set of keys. "Hey, give me a little credit, will ya?"

Outside, it had started to snow and Jamie kept the Saab's pace to a crawl down Route 3. He recognized Jen walking on the side of the road just before the intersection with 112, the Kancamagus Highway. She kept her face low to shield it from the snow. Her feet moved unsteadily along the slick pavement.

Jamie popped on his flashers and slid the passenger side window down. "Need a lift?"

Jen kept going. "It's a nice night for a walk."

"Until somebody skids into you. The Kanc's not safe tonight," Jamie said. He reached over and threw open the passenger door. "Get in."

She stopped walking. "You talked me into it."

Jamie flipped the heater up a notch, as she climbed inside and closed the door behind her, shivering. "I don't usually give rides to strangers," he said and drove off.

Jen brushed the snow from her hair, flecks of moisture

dappling the old car's leather interior. "That what I am to you?"

Jamie peered past the windshield wipers. "When you act like this, yes."

"Maybe I was disappointed about the ski lesson you haven't given me yet."

"I was busy with your brother today."

"I'd like to believe you're not wasting your time."

"Would you be happier if I was?"

Jen turned round toward the snow lines left by the rear window defroster. "Let's go back for a drink. I can finish telling you about all the ways my life is messed up."

"There are more?"

"Come on, James, we'll flip a coin. Heads, I'll wear that wire and ruin my career. Tails, I'll tell them to screw themselves and ruin my career. What do you say?"

"There's something you need to see first."

Jamie parked the car and led her along the edge of the snow-covered woods on South Mountain Road. Jen was shivering from the cold and Jamie eased an arm protectively over her. Instead of shrinking away, she tucked against him, and he felt her arm wrap around his waist.

They walked past the twinkling lights in the windows of the lodge and private homes nestled in the brush. The snow was unmarred by footprints or tire tracks, and Jamie almost felt guilty leaving a mark in the soft, rising layers. The mellow smell of wood smoke drifted through the trees, unseen yet somehow warming in its mere presence.

"This is it," he said when they reached the clearing, pointing up the steep, narrow rise of the Chute.

She stiffened and twisted back toward him. "This is *what?*"

"A trail; well, not a trail in the official sense; more like an aberration of nature. It's called the Chute."

Jen shook her head. "People actually skied down this thing?"

"A few. Matt wants to take a turn on it Sunday."

She looked at Jamie again. "You told him he was crazy, of course. You told him no."

"Actually, I didn't."

Jen's eyes flipped again to the Chute. "You're kidding, right?"

"I told Marge that Matt wanted to ski it before you leave. I asked her to go along with me, so he'd think we were really going to let him."

"In other words, you lied."

"I didn't have much choice. He told me he was going to try a run down the Chute whether I went along with it or not."

"What exactly is going to change his mind now?"

"I teach him enough to make him realize he's not ready."

"And if that doesn't work . . ."

"I have the forest rangers arrest him for trespassing." Jamie smiled, waited for Jen to join in. "That was a joke," he said, when she didn't.

"You should have just told him to forget it."

"Hasn't he heard that enough in the last few months?"

"Not from me."

"No, mostly from himself."

"You sound like you actually *want* him to ski down this thing," Jen accused, gesturing angrily toward the Chute.

And in that instant, just that instant, Jamie was sixteen again, standing at the top of the Chute ready to conquer it himself. The nervous flutter of fear in his stomach. The way his hands were jittering. He would never have turned back, not for anything. The trail was his to best alone.

But what if he hadn't been alone?

Funny, Jamie had never asked himself that question before. Now, standing at the bottom of the trail he had never reached on skis, the anomaly of how fast Cap Morgan had reached him struck again with the force of a hard fall on ice.

What if . . .

"I hope you know what you're doing," Jen was saying.

Jamie turned back toward her. "You brought him to Loon so he could feel like a whole person again."

"And that's the way I'd like to bring him home on Sunday," she snapped.

"You can trust me."

"Can I?"

"Count on Matt never skiing this trail."

"Why?"

"Because I'd have to ski it with him, and that's one thing I will absolutely never do. Once was too much."

"Good thing."

Their eyes met and Jamie could almost see the fire in Jen's, hot enough to keep her warm in the harsh cold of the snowy night.

Jamie didn't know which of them moved first, but suddenly his lips were pressed against Jen's, their bodies locked in an embrace tighter than any he had ever felt, even in his years with Meg. It all happened so fast that he didn't have time to think.

They dropped knees first into the snow, crunching the thick base and flattening it out beneath them. Jamie could feel Jen's hands, his hands. Moving, feeling, probing.

The cold was there, surrounding them, but it seemed to be retreating as they sank further into the snow. He could feel the feathery touch of the flakes on the back of his neck before they turned to water against his hot skin.

They were almost buried in the snow when Jamie raked

the zipper of Jen's ski jacket down and found her breasts through a thick wool pullover. He felt Jen reach for his ski pants and went for her jeans, the powdery snow melting as it touched them.

The cold vanished the instant he eased himself inside her, the snow turned into a heat blanket beneath them. He pulled his gloves off with his teeth so he could run his hands through her hair. It was damp with the falling snow that had left melting crystals on her brow. He licked them away, tasting her, feeling the warmth spreading between the two of them.

The feel of the soft flakes drew them reluctantly back to the world. Jamie felt a profound peace spread though him; in that moment, he could have been anyone, gone anywhere.

But his gaze drifted up the base of the Chute and he decided to be himself, go back eight years to the first and only time he had skied the Chute. Lying broken in the cold until Cap Morgan came to his rescue. Out of nowhere. Ahead of everyone else.

"Jamie?"

He heard Jen speak his name, felt her hug him tight. But he was gone, far away, lost in a truth that had finally dawned on him.

CHAPTER TWENTY-SEVEN

Cap Morgan was waiting when Jamie walked into the adaptive ski school headquarters first thing Thursday morning. Cap looked over at him and tried very hard to smile.

"You got a few minutes, son?"

"As many as you like."

The way Jamie said that must have unnerved Cap, because something changed in his expression.

"Midge said we could use her office," he said.

Jamie entered first.

Cap followed him in. "You been here three months, I've seen you, what, all of ten minutes."

"Things get pretty busy around here. You warned me about that."

"I did, didn't I? Well, I don't mind telling you you've made me look pretty good. Midge didn't think you'd last a week when I brought you over."

"I never really thanked you for that. Everything else, too."

In that instant, the old Cap came alive. "Don't mention it."

"No, I want to. It's important that I do. In fact, I was going to come see you today."

"I guess I beat you to it."

"Saved me the trouble."

Cap sat down on Marge's desk. "Look, what I got to say isn't easy."

"Me either."

"I want to talk to you about last night."

"A little more recent than what I had in mind."

Cap was nodding, seeming not to hear him, not paying attention. The smile stayed behind his lips, out of reach. "Quite a stunt you guys pulled, if you don't mind me saying."

"You just did. Now tell me why you bothered."

"Those five kids—"

"Assholes."

"I won't disagree with you there, son. They deserved what you boys did to them. They had it coming and they know it."

"Why does it matter to you?"

"Because I'm their coach, son. That's the New England champion open-division ski team you messed with."

Everything clicked into place for Jamie, like the final pieces of a jigsaw puzzle finally revealing the whole picture.

"Thing is," he said, "they messed with us first."

"They admitted that to me."

"Noble of them."

"And they're willing to make full restitution for all the damage they did in here."

"I'd rather see them eat Gus's old mono ski."

Cap popped off the desk and stood up stiffly. "That kind of talk's not going to get us anywhere."

"What kind of talk would you prefer?"

"Something bothering you?"

"You defending these bastards, for starters."

"I'm not defending them."

"Protecting, then."

"I'm just trying to set things right. That's why I'm here."

"A truce, I suppose, is what you're after."

"Right."

"Wrong, Cap. It won't work."

Cap looked at him for a long moment and for the first time Jamie saw a forty-year-old man who couldn't hold on to his youth but was afraid to let go. Pathetic in the same sense it could have been deemed attractive. "I figure you're even, squared up. They pay for the damage they did in here, and this can end right now."

"Good team?"

"As good as I've ever had."

"Nice bunch of guys?"

"They're fine on the slopes."

"Like me." Jamie wasn't sure until that instant he was going to be able to go through with this. "Or what I could have been if I hadn't left a few chunks of my leg on the Chute that day. Boy, if you hadn't come along when you did . . ."

Cap shrugged, *Don't mention it* written all over his expression.

"How'd you get there so fast, Cap?"

Before Cap could form an answer, Jamie started up again.

"You got to me so fast because you were watching. You were standing in the woods watching the whole thing happen. Because it was you who told me about the Chute. It was you who told me about all the great ones who had cut their teeth on it. You dared me to ski it, you *wanted* me to ski it. And then you sat back and watched like it was a scene out of a movie."

Cap didn't say a word, didn't even move. His eyes drooped a little and his shoulders slumped. That was all.

"You think anything you'd done up until that point really meant anything?" he asked suddenly, a stranger standing before Jamie now. "You really think you could have gone anywhere if you couldn't handle a trail by yourself without anyone holding a stopwatch? Goddammit, I did it for you!"

"You did it for me to see whether I was worth the effort or not."

A thin smile crossed Cap's lips. "Word is one of your adaptive students wants to take a turn on the Chute. You gonna let him?"

Jamie said nothing.

"You let him, try explaining the difference between you and me."

"The difference is even if I hadn't busted up my leg, you would have moved on to some other speed skier. Like those college boys you've got now, maybe."

Cap straightened back up a little. "You wanted the Olympics, son. I was trying to get you there."

"You were trying to get yourself there. You've been trying for fifteen years, and you haven't found a skier who's even gotten you close."

"That could be about to change."

"Those college guys?"

"One of them, Goldy."

"How good is he?"

"You want to find out?" asked a voice from the door.

Jamie turned and recognized the tall, lanky blond kid who had started all the trouble by going for a chair in Woodstock Station Monday night. Goldy, no doubt.

"Come on, what do you say?" Goldy continued. "A match race tomorrow, just you and me. Settle this once and for all. See if you've still got it or not."

Jamie's heart was pounding against his chest and his mouth had gone bone dry. "Sounds good," he said before he really thought about it.

Cap fixed his eyes like a gun sight on Jamie's bad leg. "A

match race on a competition trail?" He shook his head. "You have absolutely lost your mind, son."

Jamie was still staring at the blond-haired kid. "We'll see."

Jamie watched them leave, figuring Cap had made a good point about his leg, a very good point. What was he thinking? He should have backed down, rejected Goldy's challenge flat. But he couldn't.

Since even a leisurely instructor's pace had sent him for ice and Advil on a regular basis, the prospects of a race down Loon's top competition trail was daunting indeed. His leg was tight and sore already, the slightest bit of overexertion making it feel like somebody was sandpapering away on the inside. And now he had committed himself to something that could cripple him for life. There was only one person who might be able to help him.

Jamie had seen Merlin work his magic so often in the past three months it had become routine. From custom fitting outriggers for a young child, to altering equipment to the specific abilities (not *dis*abilities, Marge was always fond of saying) of a student, to repairing all the equipment Goldy and his gang had trashed two nights before, Merlin *was* a magician.

He was on the shy side of sixty with the look of a next-door neighbor always ready with a wave. He was almost totally bald and wore blue work pants and suspenders under a thick down coat to work. After arriving at the school headquarters, he would slide through the bustle unnoticed to his closet-sized room, replace his down coat with an apron, and set to work breathing life into steel, rubber, and plastic.

"What exactly do you need?" Merlin asked.

"It's kind of hard to put into words. . . ."

"Describe the injury, the limitations, the other kinds of equipment you've tried."

Jamie considered responses for all three, then sighed and pulled up his ski pants to expose the scars on his bad leg instead.

Merlin inspected it, his callused, craftsman's hands already planning things out. "Shouldn't be a problem."

"What about for downhill?"

Merlin didn't miss a beat. "That's a problem." He backed off toward his tool table. "When do you need it by?"

"Tomorrow afternoon."

Merlin didn't even look up from his table. He simply dug out some measuring tools and went back to scutinizing Jamie's leg.

"Now, just hold still . . ."

"Can I ask you a question?"

"Sure," Merlin said a bit distantly, continuing with his work.

"How'd you get so good at this?"

"Always had a knack for inventing things, I guess."

"I heard you were a retired engineer or something."

"Close enough."

"Any of your inventions work out?"

"You know those parabolic skis everyone's finally gotten around to using?"

"Sure," said Jamie.

Merlin finally looked back up at him. "That's one."

FIVE

CHAPTER TWENTY-EIGHT

"What are we gonna do today?" Matt asked, as they walked outside into the lightly falling snow early on Friday morning.

"We'll run the harder intermediate trails," Jamie said, finding it hard to concentrate on teaching. "Move on to advanced parallel turns and short swings from there."

Matt rolled his eyes. "We did advanced parallel turns yesterday afternoon. You forget?"

Jamie realized he had. All of yesterday was a blur from the time Merlin completed the fitting for the brace he now wore on his leg. It was actually more a sleeve than a brace. Merlin had started with a broken knee stabilizer normally used to restrict motion as a rehab tool for those recovering from surgery and a brace for those who didn't want to undergo it. To this he had added a tubular attachment that ran the length of Jamie's once-shattered leg bone. The attachment fit snugly under his ski pants and extended all the way down into the ski boot, where it hooked under the heel.

Merlin had to adjust the fit a little, leaving it a little tight. Then he made Jamie imitate the motions most likely to reinjure the leg. Jamie tried them all and felt the brace grab hold each time, right before the pain would otherwise have taken over. He had skied with it already, tentatively at first, but had already gotten used to the brace's feel and bulk.

"Refresh my memory," Jamie said to Matt, pulling his mind away from the match race, just a few hours off now.

"Outrigger like a pole," Matt started.

"It's coming back to me . . ."

"Flip-ski down, I touch the left lightly on the snow . . ."

"That's right, yeah, lightly."

". . . while I raise the other up like this."

Matt exaggerated the motion, elongating it into something out of ballet. "That brings me to the left, until I reverse the motion, right on the snow and left in the air." He turned gracefully to the right. "You remember now?"

"Vaguely."

"Something on your mind?"

"No."

"Liar."

"I'm going to race this afternoon."

Saying it aloud surprised him as much as it did Matt, because Jamie had no intention of telling anyone who didn't have to know.

Matt stared at him. "Those days were long gone, I thought you said."

"I changed my mind," Jamie said.

Matt's eyes turned to needles, poking at him. "If you can run a race, I can run the Chute."

Jamie had been waiting for Matt outside the lodge after lunch when Jen showed up with a pair of skis held awkwardly on her shoulder. She walked in her ski boots as if she expected to fall, never far from the wall in case she needed to reach out and grab hold.

"Matt's asleep," she explained. "I didn't want to wake him up yet, so I thought I'd just come instead."

"Good idea."

"So let's go. See how good you are. See if you can get me ready to ski the Chute by Sunday, too."

They started in the soft patch of level snow just to the right of the lodge, Jen starting to fall the moment Jamie helped her click her boots into her rental skis. The wind tousled her hair; a stubborn strand blew onto her face that Jen kept brushing away only to have it return. She gave up and smiled.

At first he tried to be patient and understanding with her. Then he went through a brief stage of frustration with Jen's utter ineptitude, to the point where he could feel himself getting angry. Jen got mad too, resolved to show him up, and ended up skiing across the sidewalk into the fence line when Jamie couldn't stop her in time.

"I think we better move away from anything solid," he said, guiding her to Sarsaparilla, where they moved on to wedge turns.

Finally, when she tried to stop herself and ended up sliding slowly right off the trail, he started laughing.

"Think it's funny?" she said from the snow, as he helped her up. "Fine. I quit."

And with that she tossed aside the poles she was holding mainly as ornanents and stormed off—well, at least she *started* to storm off, having forgotten that the skis that were the source of her problems were still fastened to her feet. Jen went down even harder in a clump and Jamie broke out laughing again.

Jen joined in and before long he was sitting in the snow next to her, kissing her lightly on the lips as beginners skied past them.

"That's the only place it doesn't hurt," she told him.

"The lesson's not over yet."

"Oh yes, it is."

She tried to get back to her feet, failed, and they laughed some more.

"You going to help me up?"

"I'm enjoying this."

"That's why I went out and spent a hundred dollars renting all this equipment—to give you a good time."

He shook his head and waved a reproaching finger at her. "You didn't have to spend a hundred bucks to give me a good time."

"I thought maybe I did, after I didn't hear from you last night."

"I had a lot on my mind."

"The race this afternoon?"

"You heard."

"I heard. Not from you, obviously."

"I was afraid you'd try to talk me out of it."

"It doesn't make a lot of sense, under the circumstances."

"Which ones?" Jamie asked her.

"You can't win and you may hurt yourself trying."

"I have to do this. I don't know why, but I have to."

"Macho bullshit, if you ask me," Jen said.

"Like you refusing to wear a wire for the Feds, even though it might cost you your career?"

"I don't think you can really compare the two."

"I think you can. They're both about making a stand, going as far as you can before you have to draw the line."

"I'm just trying to make a point, James, not a stand."

"The point that you're not going to let anyone push you around anymore."

"And who's pushing you around? Who's got you backed into a corner and is forcing you to race? This kid challenged you and you didn't want to back down. Right or wrong?"

Jamie sat up. "Right," he said, sounding like it was the first time he had thought of it that way. "It would have been easy to say no, but I've always done the easy thing, right up until three months ago when I ended up here."

"Like me using drugs?"

"Only if it's harder without them. That's why your decision not to wear a wire isn't about the Feds or your bosses—it's about you."

"So the two of us come up here and find each other." Jen smiled. "And I thought it was opposites that attract."

"Good thing," said Jamie, "that's not always the case."

"When were you going to tell me about this race?" Marge asked Jamie after he returned to the school alone.

"I wasn't."

"Didn't think you needed my permission?"

"No, I figured I did. That's why I didn't say anything."

"You also weren't straight with me on the damage to your leg."

"How'd you find out?"

"The drawings of that brace Merlin made for you. Belonged to somebody on the other side of the adaptive program—that's what I thought when I saw them."

"But you talked to Cap too, right?"

"He informed me he was going along with this match race against his better judgment. Because of your leg."

"You believe his concern was genuine?"

"Hell no, hotshot. I'm pretty certain he wanted me to call it off out of anything *but* concern. I was all set to put an end to these shenanigans, as a matter of fact, until he stopped by. Now I'm letting you ski."

"He apologize for what his team did?"

"Profusely."

"But not until after I confronted him about it."

"That's another reason why I'm letting this farce go for-

ward. I don't know what it is the two of you got going between you, but it's clear whatever it is didn't start the other
night at Woodstock Station."

"You're right about that."

"Can I give you the 'put it behind you' speech now?"

"I have put it behind me."

"So this isn't about revenge?"

"In part it is. Not against Cap, though. What Goldy and
his friends did to this place—this is the best way to make
them pay."

"Freezing them solid wasn't enough?"

Jamie shook his head. "Lasted only until they took a hot
bath."

"And what if you're the one who ends up paying? What if
Merlin's contraption doesn't work?"

"I can handle it."

"Emotionally, maybe. What about physically? You really
think you're up to another month in the hospital? Recon-
structive surgery, bone grafts, crutches, a walker, a cane."

"I know the progression, Midge."

"And I know what the doctors told you about skiing
again, never mind competitively. You snap that same leg today
and you *will* end up on the other side of the program, I shit
you not."

"You going to be at the race?"

"Cheering my loudest."

CHAPTER TWENTY-NINE

"Catch my snow, asshole," Goldy grinned, looking up from a final check of his skis at the top of Rumrunner.

Jamie fixed his eyes on him until Goldy broke the stare, like a pair of prizefighters in the ring. His skis felt a little tight beneath him. They weren't the best kind for downhill racing, too short, but Jamie was used to them and today was the wrong time for a change.

"You guys ready?" asked the instructor who'd be starting the race.

They both nodded. The best of the skiing was long done for the day and the light had already started to fade from the sky. Cap had managed to close Rumrunner down early, but the hours of constant pounding had nonetheless left it very icy, which was exactly what Jamie was counting on.

"Okay, then, here we go. . . ."

Jamie lowered his goggles into place and took another look at Goldy. His best times beat Jamie's from eight years ago by over three seconds, meaning the race shouldn't even be close. But he was cocky and arrogant, and Jamie was counting on that to help lead to the younger man's undoing.

After all, racing a person was considerably different than racing a clock. All competitive skiers approached a trail with a specific agenda and strategy, to be adjusted accordingly by the conditions of the weather and the terrain. You had a plan and you stuck to it. If Jamie could make Goldy deviate from his, even in the slightest, he would have a chance.

As for the rest of Goldy's undoing, Jamie would have to rely on a strategy fraught with risk. Success or failure would come down to a single moment on the course, and that was the best he could hope for under the circumstances.

"On your mark," the starter began, taking his position.

Jamie bent at the knees and squared his shoulders. He tried to angle his whole body forward to assure a strong start. Fingers tight on the pole handles now, ready to push off. One way or another, it would all be over in barely two minutes.

"Get set!"

Jamie got his poles into position, rocked his skis back and forth on the surface of the snow.

"*Go . . .*"

The word echoed in Jamie's head as he pushed off and hit the trail hard, gaining speed fast down the slope. In that instant he felt sixteen years old again, shaving seconds from his time the only thing that mattered. But the feeling lasted only for that instant. Today he was racing down an icy trail with a leg bound by a brace salvaged from the garbage against a champion skier with the Olympics as his goal.

Jamie glanced at Goldy and noted he had come out of the gate in the lead and was doing everything he could to extend it before Jamie caught hold of the snow. It was even icier than he had expected, having been melted and instantly refrozen beneath hundreds of skis over the previous seven hours. All of the neighboring trails were empty as well now, and the only sound Jamie could hear besides the wind and the slice of his skis was the roar of the snow guns spraying white clouds into the air across the mountain.

Having taken an early lead, Goldy was certain to be more cautious into the turns. Take them a little wider and cut back more uphill to stay in control, anything to avoid the worst patches of ice. Jamie intended to make that work for him, along with the ice. Ice was treacherous but it was also fast, and Jamie would need that speed if his plan were to work.

Merlin's brace was holding up well, as he whirled into the first of the trail's sharp turns. He cut it closer and less wide than Goldy, and the result was to slice the gap between them in half. Jamie could see Goldy stealing a glance behind him, perhaps surprised Jamie was still there and definitely surprised that he was as close as he was.

Goldy narrowed and quickened his turns, shrinking the trail, but Jamie skied close enough to the ruts to hold his ground. He worked his poles faster, shifting his hips smoothly from side to side, and kept Goldy from pulling away.

They rocketed into a straightaway still twenty-five feet apart, Jamie tucking as low as Merlin's leg brace would allow him to go as he snapped his poles under his arms. His ski tips were close and straight and they made a whining sound over the snow, which was so icy it gleamed.

Jamie whizzed by one of the control gates, angling left. Then he straightened and worked his poles again when the course curved sharply down the slope of the mountain. He could hear himself instructing Matt on the very maneuvers he was executing himself now, but they weren't bringing him any closer to Goldy.

The kid might be an asshole, but he was damn good at downhill. All elbows and joints, too lanky to be a skier at first glance, he knew how to coil his frame and work the air.

They approached the halfway point where the course bent on to another trail called Coolidge Street, and Jamie took the next turn over the ice without reducing his speed. He felt his skis start to slide, but strained to keep the tips even and held fast. The maneuver cut Goldy's lead to barely ten feet. He glanced over his shoulder again, clearly shocked by how close Jamie had drawn. He wobbled slightly on his skis and, in the seconds it took him to restore his balance, Jamie had closed the gap to a mere two yards.

Just ahead of him, he could see Goldy stiffen, but the kid didn't grasp the worst of it yet: that Jamie was close enough now to ride his slipstream, tucking in behind him and letting his opponent's speed work for both of them. Staying close enough to give himself the one chance he needed.

They came out of another straightaway as a single dark blur against the white. Jamie rode Goldy's back, feeling the spray of crystalized snow stinging his face.

Suddenly Goldy slowed, ever so slightly but enough for Jamie to draw almost even with him. Before Jamie could gauge his intent, Goldy lashed a pole back against him. It caught Jamie on his bad leg, and he wavered but didn't slow, thanks to the magic of Merlin's brace.

Goldy snapped the pole out again and a burst of pain exploded just below Jamie's knee. He fought the temptation to strike back, knowing that Goldy was now giving him just the opportunity he had been hoping for.

They rode the mountain side by side, jackets almost touching. Goldy kept jabbing and poking with his pole, hammering the boot with it now.

Jamie felt stabs of pain that he swallowed gratefully as the sharp whiplash turn just before the final straightaway came within view. He bit his lip, his bad leg starting to shake from the pounding it had taken. He watched Goldy start to pull confidently away again, prepared to execute the turn that would take him to victory.

Jamie took a deep breath; he had gotten his chance, couldn't ask for any more than that.

Goldy cut into his turn first.

But Jamie took his own at a complete right angle, going out wide and cutting diagonally across the trail instead of riding the hill. His whole body was trembling and, for a long second at least, he was out of control, clinging to the hope his skis would hold the icy surface long enough for him to come out of the turn safely.

The maneuver sliced him across Goldy's path, coming so close that their skis touched and Jamie's left one popped free. The pounding his bad leg had taken from Goldy's pole must have loosened its binding. Jamie was ready to fall, *expected* to fall, but he didn't. He angled into the final straightaway without missing a beat, holding a slight lead, skiing on his one remaining ski.

In that instant everything he had taught Matt, every drill and maneuver they had practiced, came back to him. He kept his free leg curled behind him as he squatted down on the one still in his ski and tucked himself low. He shot his poles back under his arms like darts, nothing to see before him but snow and the crowds gathered before the base lodge.

Jamie could feel himself picking up incredible speed down the straightaway, could hear Goldy drawing closer, almost even, over the roar of the nearby snow guns and cheers of those clustered in a U at the end of the trail. But Goldy's tips got only as far as the center of Jamie's remaining ski before the two skiers crossed the finish line and soared past the gallery along the fence line.

Faces flew by, far more spectators watching the race than he had thought originally. Jed and Beth and Gus and Frank Rawley hurried after him. Jamie caught a glimpse of Marge hovering near the back; smiling, he was pretty sure. He steered to a leisurely stop and felt slaps on the back, hearty congratulations from people he had never seen before. And not far off he could hear Goldy screaming to a pair of instructors-turned-judges about the illegal turn that had propelled Jamie ahead of him into the straightaway. The instructors were hearing none of it. Cap Morgan, meanwhile, was nowhere to be seen.

Jamie turned and saw Matt and Jen hurrying toward him.

"Not bad for a two-legged guy," Matt said. "I guess you were pretty good, after all."

"Was?" Jamie asked, wrapping his arm around Jen. "Think you can do better?"

"That a challenge?"

"Depends if you're up for it."

"Try me."

"Tomorrow morning: we try a diamond."

Matt smirked. "Can't you do any better than that?"

CHAPTER THIRTY

First thing Saturday Jamie and Matt rode the Gondola to the summit of the mountain and tried a black-diamond trail called Big Dipper. They moved to Flume after that, and then Walking Boss, running the gamut of Loon's most challenging trails.

By the third run, Jamie could see all they'd been working on falling into place. Short swings were the last technique Matt needed to nail, the key being to keep his upper body centered over the ski, while his leg moved from side to side. This morning, for the first time, every time Matt started to sway, Jamie could sense him recall the feeling of centering himself on the board he'd been practicing on in the gym to hold steady. His outriggers got lighter and lighter, as he shifted weight from the left to the right and back again, holding his balance out of even the steepest turns.

The boy nailed all his turns and, by the fourth run, his balance had stopped wavering. A single fall on the Dipper was the only setback, and even this Matt handled well, not panicking when his ski separated and using the outriggers to stop his slide from becoming a tumble.

Marge skied along for their fifth run and didn't bother to hide her surprise and satisfaction.

"Five days and you've got him skiing diamonds?"

"He's got himself doing it. I just helped out a little."

"I'm tempted to pull out my watch. This kid could be a racer, I shit you not. How in the hell did you pull this off?"

"Beginner's luck."

Marge's eyes lit up devilishly. "No. You let him have the Chute, a goal that made everything else pale by comparison. He's doing the impossible and he doesn't even realize it because he wants more."

"Did I do all that?"

She moved a little closer. "Just check your ego long enough to tell me something else: is he still expecting to ski the Chute tomorrow?"

"Right now, yes."

"Like taking things down to the wire, don't you?"

"It's something I'm used to."

Jamie had expected all along that jumps would be what stopped Matt in his tracks. After only five days three-tracking, jumps would provide the dose of reality the boy needed to realize he wasn't ready for the Chute, especially after getting six, eight, or even more feet of air.

Jamie watched Matt make out fine off the first small moguls they tackled, but anything after four feet of air turned his landings to mush. He fell hard again and again, but refused to quit, refused to give in. Jamie winced harder with each fall, feeling the thuds as much as Matt did.

Because Jamie had quit once himself, he had given in. That's what had brought him up here. And, in that instant, it seemed that if he didn't help this boy, it would all have been for nothing. He would be back where he started. Afraid to grow up, just as Meg had hinted. Incapable of handling the responsibilities that mattered most, just as Marge had said.

Finally, Matt tossed his outriggers aside and slammed the snow with his palms.

"It's the same!" he raged, half sobbing.

Jamie knelt next to him. "Same as what?"

"Everything! Kicking a soccer ball. I tried and I can't do it anymore. Why should this be any different?"

Jamie watched Matt look down and cover his face with his hands. Ready to quit. Jamie knew he couldn't let him, not like this, because he knew better than anyone what that felt like.

"It's different because I'm here," Jamie said. "You ready to start listening again?"

"Just leave me alone."

"If I had done that when you asked me five days ago, we wouldn't be here now, would we?"

Matt moved his hands away from his face. "A lot of good it's doing me."

"There's no way you can avoid jumps on a trail like the Chute, or any double black diamond for that matter. Try to avoid them on a trail with a grade that steep and all you'll do is crash and burn. The thing is to be ready and know what to do when you come out of the jump so you don't spill."

Matt looked up at him. "Which is?"

"You want to minimize your air. The more air you get, the harder your landing, and you can't afford tough landings on the Chute."

"So how can I hold my air down?"

"First, pop your ski off. I want to try something."

Matt did as he was told.

"Okay," Jamie said, backing maybe ten feet away from him, "I want you to broad jump straight for me."

Matt crouched low on his leg and pushed himself upward, landing in a neat tuck just in front of Jamie.

"You got low to get into your jump."

"Of course. How else would I do it?"

"It's the same motion you use when you take a mogul.

You feel your ski going over it and you tuck up low, then lift upward at the peak to generate lift. Absorb the jump and you'll get less air. Makes for easier landings."

"Like this," Matt said, before he broad jumped back in the opposite direction, exaggerating the motion of landing.

"Exactly. Except, remember, on the Chute you're going to be in motion again as soon as you touch down."

"You got a way to teach me what to do about that?"

Jamie nodded. "As a matter of fact, I do."

Jamie dug out a twelve-foot tether from his backpack and looped it around the front tip of Matt's ski. This time, when the boy took his first jumps, Jamie pulled on the tether gently, seeming to guide him down.

"Like training wheels," he explained, "to make sure you come out of the jump angled toward the center of the slope. That way you hit the trail sideways and maintain control. A few more and then we take the training wheels off."

Except those training wheels had never gone on. Jamie wasn't really doing anything with the tether, other than supplying Matt with confidence. And once the boy had built that confidence on his own, Jamie had him take jumps of all sizes, building a little at a time without the tether. The boy did better and better until he soared toward a muffin-shaped mogul that rose a good four feet off the ground. Jamie could see his approach was all wrong and clung to the hope Matt would veer away at the last. But Matt didn't and turned sideways in the air, hitting the snow on the other side as Jamie hurried to reach him.

"It's my leg," the boy winced.

"Which one?" Jamie asked, kneeling down alongside him.

"Very funny."

Matt had landed with his leg twisted slightly beneath him.

After the boy was able to ease the leg out, Jamie helped him straighten it and checked for obvious injury.

"Ow!"

"I think you sprained your ankle."

"Help me up."

"We should get the ski patrol."

"Help me up. I've had enough of stretchers and ambulances."

Jamie hoisted Matt to his feet and then looped his head under the boy's shoulder to support him.

Matt stiffened. "I can make it back on my own."

"Don't be stubborn."

Matt pulled away from him, and his leg almost buckled again. "Just stay close to me."

They skied off slowly, Matt transferring as much of his weight as he could to his outriggers. A grimace stretched across his face the whole way back, but Matt didn't stop once, nor did he fall.

Back at the adaptive school headquarters, another instructor who was a doctor had Matt lie down on a bench and gave his ankle a thorough examination.

"There's a little swelling, so it's only a minor sprain. You'll be skiing again next weekend."

"Not tomorrow?"

The doctor shook his head. "Not tomorrow. I'll tape it up and then we'll find you a pair of crutches. . . ."

When the doctor was finished, Matt sat up and dabbed his eyes with a sleeve.

Jamie sat down across from him, relieved that the task of finding a way to stop Matt from skiing the Chute would no longer fall to him. "I'm sorry."

"It wasn't your fault."

"If it's worth anything, I think you could have done it. I think you could have handled the Chute."

Matt looked over at him. "It's not worth enough."

"The Chute will still be here next time."

"Maybe I'll come back. See what other parts of me I can mess up until I run out of limbs." Something in Matt's face changed. "You didn't want me to ski it, did you?"

"I've been there. I know what happens if you fail. It's not like kicking a soccer ball."

"Yes, it is." Matt straightened his shoulders against the wall supporting them. "Plenty of three trackers ski diamonds. You told me that."

"Right from the start. That was the point."

"Ever heard of a three-tracker skiing the Chute?"

"Absolutely not."

"*That's* the point," said Matt.

CHAPTER THIRTY-ONE

They ordered dinner from room service, but Matt barely touched his hamburger and fries. Jen pushed him into choosing a movie off the pay service, and he hardly watched it, finally dozing off on the couch in the suite's living room.

She switched off the television and lights while Jamie made sure Matt's leg was elevated properly atop two pillows. Then the two of them walked hand-in-hand into the bedroom, where they sat together at the foot of the bed.

"You travel in style," Jamie said, impressed by the size and furnishings of the suite.

"I figured what the hell? I had some cash saved up from office pools."

"Office pools?"

"Forget about these assistant district attorneys who never met a plea bargain they didn't like, James. I used to put people away for real. We kept a running tab in the office of total years of incarceration. I won two years in a row."

"Congratulations."

"Streak got broken this year," Jen said. "I looked across the court at the people I was prosecuting and started seeing them as somebody's husband or wife, daughter or son. People with a family. What good will it do to put them away? Who does it really serve? You put somebody in jail, you're not just punishing them. They got a kid, what happens to him or her while they're inside for two years with good behavior? Two years is a lifetime. Lives get changed."

"It doesn't have to take *that* long."

"So I start seeing the people they left behind, start obsessing about what they're doing day by day. You see what I'm saying? I used to collect the years all the sentences amounted to. Now I collect the people left behind by the ones I put away. I check up on them. Call occasionally. The ones who talk to me don't usually have a lot of nice things to say."

"You can't really blame them."

"I don't," Jen said softly and her eyes drifted to the open door leading back to the living area of the suite where her brother was sleeping. "I guess I should be relieved about Matt."

"You got what you wanted."

"This isn't the way I wanted it to happen."

"It happened."

She looked at him incredulously. "You sound like you think we should have let him ski the Chute."

"Do you remember what brought you up here?"

"I had to show Matt there was something he could do as well as he used to."

"As well."

"Yes, and he did. That's good enough for me."

"Maybe it's not good enough for Matt. You look at him and want him to realize he can still be who he was. But he's not that person anymore, Jen. That person got left behind at the accident. And while you're doing everything you can to get Matt back to himself, he decided to start all over again. It's a longer route, but ultimately it's easier to see where you're going."

"How do *you* know?"

"I didn't—until just now. But I think that's what I've been doing here at Loon all along, just like Matt has. It's what we needed."

"Matt didn't need the Chute."

"Not the old Matt."

Jen could feel her skin start to prickle with a sudden angry warmth. "If you feel that way, why don't you go ski the damn trail?"

"This isn't about me, remember?" Jamie said, and she looked away.

They never took off their clothes that night, or even climbed under the covers. Just lay atop the bed next to each other.

"What happens when you get home?" Jamie asked, after an uncomfortable silence when both of them wondered if he was going to leave.

"He'll go back to school on Monday."

"I wasn't talking about Matt."

"I think I'm going to tell my boss to shove it."

"In those words?"

"Close enough. I'm not going to wear any wire, and I'm not going to let them use me. This happened three months ago. If they were going to fire me, they would have done it already. But they can't, because it would make the office look like shit. A scandal's the last thing they need."

"So you quit, and get a better job in private practice."

"It'll be tough to ask for references." Jen took a deep breath. "I walk away from this and my bosses will do everything they can to ruin me behind the scenes, where it matters."

"You'll have to prove them wrong."

"If somebody gives me a chance. I'm not counting on it,

and I'm not even saying I deserve it. We'll see what happens."

"You don't sound scared."

"I've been scared long enough," Jen said.

They finally drifted off to sleep to the flutter of snow against the window, a smattering of house lights twinkling in the naked woods beyond the room's undrawn blinds. They couldn't have slept long, but Jen could never remember a deeper, more satisfying rest.

She awoke to a soft thunking sound to find the sun struggling to push through a gray sky aglow with falling snowflakes.

What had she heard?

She pushed herself to her feet and straightened her sweater, then moved to check on Matt.

Halfway through the door, she stopped cold, blinking a few times to make sure the dimmer light in the living room section of the suite hadn't deceived her. But she knew it hadn't, just as she knew now what the sound that had awoken her must have been.

She hurried back into the bedroom, shaking as she leaned over to rouse Jamie.

"Matt's gone," Jen said when he opened his eyes and looked up at her.

CHAPTER THIRTY-TWO

"He's going to try this bad ankle and all, isn't he?" Jen managed, through the clog in her throat.

Jamie tossed the tape Matt had stripped off his leg back to the couch. "I don't think he hurt his ankle at all; I think he tricked us."

"To ski the Chute."

"So nobody would stop him, talk him out of it."

"My God."

They rushed along the slope line toward the Governor Adams Base Lodge and the adaptive ski school on the other side of the complex. Above them the stilled chairlifts swayed eerily in the wind, creaking, seats coated with neat cushions of white. The roar of the snow guns making the last of the night's snow shattered the peace of the morning and made it difficult for them to hear each other as they ran.

"The ski Matt's been using is gone," Jamie said, inside the adaptive ski school.

"We've got to call the ski patrol!" Jen insisted.

"They're not on duty yet," Jamie told her and snatched his own skis off the rack.

"What are you doing?"

"Going after him."

*   *   *

Matt stood at the top of the Chute, poised on his outriggers. One push and he'd be off. One push and everyone else could be damned.

His stomach fluttered. He knew the moderate grade at the Chute's outset was deceiving; by the time the first turn passed, gazing down the trail would feel like standing at the window of a high-rise. The sheer drop was a breath-stealing sight. The view was like that from a roller coaster, only you weren't belted in for the ride with a safety bar before you.

He thought this last exhilarating moment would be the easy part, but he couldn't move. He didn't feel exhilarated; he felt alone and it scared him. One moment had shattered his entire life, and he kept trying to put things back together a little at a time.

Maybe, though, things came together the same way they came apart: in a single moment. And, this time, the moment was his to control. Turn around and retrace his path away from south mountain, past the DANGER and NO TRESPASSING signs, and he would lose that moment, maybe forever.

Matt shivered. His good leg trembled, shifting the ski slightly. He thought he heard someone calling his name, but he was in motion by then, coasting into the wind.

"Matt!"

Jamie emerged from the woods near the top of the trail, just as Matt's shape disappeared from sight around the first bend. Instead of taking off after the boy, he hesitated and looked forward into the blowing snow.

He had stood in almost this very spot once before, eight years ago. It had been a sunlit day, and Jamie remembered looking out over the entire expanse of the White Mountains

from the top of the trail. Today that view had been closed off
by the squall, the world reduced to the dimensions of the
Chute and no more. Somehow that made the trail seem even
more foreboding and ominous. Maybe Cap was right. Maybe
the Chute had proven Jamie wasn't as good as he thought he
was.

The spot where he had acknowledged this lay before him,
threatening to destroy him again. But Matt was somewhere
out there too, and Jamie pushed off, gathering speed fast.

Matt swooped out of the Chute's first turn, his ski slicing the
snow as if rails had been fitted for it. He angled sharply from
side to side and worked his outriggers like extensions of his
arms. Each twist of his body brought him more in touch with
the slope. He was moving so fast that the freshly falling snow
barely grazed his skin. A tunnel seemed to open in the center
of the squall and Matt whizzed through it, just him and the
trail, the world in front of him reduced to a white sheen.

He imagined his freshly carved tracks already disappearing
behind him, gone like the rest of his past. Three months of living uphill and now he realized what this run, what the Chute,
was all about; what he was really racing.

The first mogul came up before he could prepare for it. He
sucked his breath in and felt his ski top out at its crest, remembered to tuck as he soared through the falling flakes between the rocks and the tree line.

Jamie watched Matt hit his first jump from a hundred feet
back. He could tell the boy wasn't ready for it by the way he
came up too fast at the peak. Too high, drawing too much air,
but then tucking in midflight and landing soft and fluid.

Thank God . . .

Merlin's brace saved Jamie yet again, as he rocketed into a jump, adjusting his skis in a midair tuck to land into the slope. But another jump reared up as soon as he straightened, and Jamie grabbed eight feet of air, tensing a little as he came down and feeling his bad leg wobble in spite of the brace. He righted himself and skied on, realizing he was coming to the place where the Chute had betrayed him eight years before. He skied on, past the spot, past the person he had left here the last time.

The slope had grown so steep that Matt became nothing more than a spray of snow barely visible in the air ahead. The poles lightened in his hands and he realized the boy was doing fine, just as he was. He could have caught up to Matt with another burst, but he didn't want to startle the boy now and cause the disaster he had come here to prevent. Angling his tips a bit to slow himself, Jamie caught a glimpse of a shape shifting about back in the trees.

A bear, he thought absurdly.

But it wasn't a bear, he realized, fixing his gaze ever so briefly on a stray figure lingering at the edge of the woods.

Not a bear. No.

Worse.

Jen saw the figures emerging from the woods above South Mountain Road. They were on skis and she recognized them all too clearly as members of the Loon ski team against whom the adaptive instructors had gone to war. She had stopped to catch her breath, having taken this route to the bottom of the Chute while Jamie followed Matt's path to the top.

She realized she was almost there when the ski team members appeared. There were four of them moving pretty fast through the storm, coming from the direction of the Chute; only the blond-haired one Jamie had raced against on Friday was missing.

What if they somehow found out Jamie had been planning to bring Matt here today?

Jen stumbled into a run down the snow-packed road, not caring if they saw her.

Jamie pushed himself to pick up speed, desperately trying to catch up with Matt. He had recognized the shape in the woods as Goldy, no doubt here to extract revenge for his humiliating defeat on another course two days before.

The trail! He must have done something to the trail!

Jamie had to reach the boy, get him to stop before he sprung whatever trap Goldy had laid, at Cap Morgan's behest no doubt. Cap, after all, had heard Jamie was planning a return to the Chute. What better way, what better place, for Morgan to settle his own account.

Jamie skied harder, but Matt remained a blur of powder before him, moving too fast. Flying.

Jamie tried to fly too. Only the ache had returned to his bad leg and the poles felt like iron bars in his hands. He had lost his rhythm and suddenly fear of the Chute crept back in. He fought the impulse to slow the squealing whir of the skis beneath him and pushed on breathlessly.

He needed to reach his speed of eight years ago, needed to recapture the clip that had left him here in a twisted pile. He felt it starting to happen, but this time it was the Jamie of the present doing it. He brushed those lost years aside like snowflakes and raced away from them, beginning to close the gap to Matt.

Jen pulled herself up the Chute. She had started by charging up the base of the slope until the angle sharpened and she found herself actually climbing, pushing with her boots and clawing through the snow using her hands to pull. She had gone too far to turn back by the time she looked down.

A rush of vertigo hit her. She felt as if she were clinging to the side of a building and scrambled on, gasping, fighting the grip of panic. She slipped a few times and flailed desperately to avoid sliding all the way to the bottom. Hard-packed snow and ice crystals scraped at her face and left it first tingling, then hot. She could feel cold wetness mixing with her perspiration.

But Jen could see the pair of figures in the snow above her now, one gaining on the other, looking almost airborne. She stood up as best she could and waved her hands, screaming for them to stop.

The wind swallowed her words and she scrambled higher, seeking firmer ground to better signal Matt and Jamie. But her boot betrayed her and sank into the deep snow. When Jen yanked it out, she lost her balance and fell. She flung her hands out to stop her slide, but the air had already claimed her, and she was falling.

It seemed like a long time before she touched snow again. And then she was rolling, tumbling, the feeling of cold hardness rotating with the feeling of nothing at all as she plummetted.

Jamie was still ten feet from Matt when he saw the figure waving frantically before them. He knew it was Jen, couldn't say how but knew it all the same, just before she disappeared into the swirling white snowfall.

"Slow down!" he screamed, finally close enough for Matt to hear him.

The boy didn't acknowledge his words, still lost in the slope.

"Stop!" Jamie yelled, skiing alongside him now.

But Matt didn't stop, didn't slow down. Jamie watched his eyes widen and followed his gaze to a figure crumpled in the snow forty feet beneath them.

"Jen!" Matt wailed, and Jamie felt the world turn cold around him again.

They reached her at the same time, twisting to a halt. Jen was lying on her back, legs straight out before her angled down hill.

Matt crouched over her.

Jen's eyelids fluttered. "I'm all right. I'm all right."

Matt moved to grasp her, but Jamie grabbed hold and held him back.

"We've got to get her out of here!" the boy snapped, pulling away and nearly losing his balance.

"It'll be faster if we get the ski patrol," Jamie said, still holding onto him, balanced awkwardly on his skis. "I'll stay with her. You go."

"Why don't you go?"

"How much first aid do you know?"

"She's okay!"

Jamie grabbed Matt's shoulders. "She's going to be. Now go! Fast!"

The boy looked back at Jen one last time and then skied off, disappearing soon after he reached the bottom of the Chute.

"I lied," Jen said, lips trembling as she looked up at Jamie.

He took his jacket off and covered her with it.

"My back . . . I, I landed on something." Her eyes looked like pale marbles. "I . . . can't feel my legs."

Jamie brushed the snow from around her, came upon a row of rocks neatly camouflaged just beneath the surface of the snow.

"Bastards," he muttered, picturing Goldy and friends laying the trap that Matt would have hit first, if not for Jen.

"What?"

"Nothing."

"I can't feel my legs," Jen repeated.

Jamie took her hand and squeezed. "Can you feel this?"

"Yes."

"That's a good sign."

"I'm scared," Jen said, shivering horribly.

He cradled himself against her, careful not to disturb her position as he kept her warm. "Try to move your feet."

Jen's features squeezed tightly as she strained. "I can't."

"You just did."

"I did?"

"Both boots. Just a little. You'll start feeling tingly in your legs next."

"I can't feel anything!"

"You will. Just a few minutes from now," Jamie reassured her, holding Jen tighter.

CHAPTER THIRTY-THREE

Jamie was standing by her bedside when Jen woke up later that day in the hospital. She looked confused for an instant, then terror gripped her as she remembered what had happened.

He reached out and took her hand. On the other side of the bed, Matt took the other.

"Easy does it," Jamie warned.

"My legs . . ." The terror receded. "I can move them."

"I told you. You brusied your spine, that's all."

"They still don't feel right."

"That's the sedative working. You'll be able to walk out of here tomorrow."

She looked at Matt and tried to smile, before turning again to Jamie. "I'm tired."

"Go back to sleep."

Jamie found Marge waiting for him in the hallway.

"You want to tell me about those rocks the ski patrol dug out of the Chute?" she asked.

"Do I need to?"

Marge shook her head. Slowly. "I seem to remember saying there'd be no easy end to this."

"So do I."

"Means I have the honor of finishing it now."

"What about me?"

"That was my next question."

"Just tell me what answer you want."

"Let's start with the one that tells me why your student's sister was trespassing on south mountain."

Jamie caught the slight glint in Marge's eyes. "She must have had her reasons."

"Good thing you and her brother caught up to her." Marge was shaking her head. "Ironic, isn't it? You talk the kid out of taking a turn on the Chute and then his sister ends up taking a spill."

"Ironic," Jamie repeated, getting the message.

"You did well with Matt. I could see it in his eyes."

"How do mine look?"

"Better than they will after I break your nose."

"Take your best shot."

"It can wait until tomorrow, hotshot."

Jamie looked away from her. "I left some unfinished business behind, somewhere else."

"Some?"

"Lots."

Marge smiled, a little sadly. "All that time and effort I invested in you . . . I'd hate to think it was wasted."

"Don't worry."

"I brought you something," Jamie said when he arrived at the hospital the next morning to find Jen sitting up in bed.

She looked briefly at the bag he was holding. "Can I ask you something first?"

"Sure."

"On the mountain, after I fell, did you really see me move my feet?"

"No."

"You lied?"

"Yes."

She laced her hands behind her head. "Another subject: those college students."

"This the lawyer in you talking?"

"I'd love to prosecute their asses."

"Marge is handling it instead."

"How?"

"They won't be skiing again. Not competitively. Not ever."

"Not exactly the death penalty."

"Close enough for them, believe me."

Jen didn't look convinced. "If Matt had skied into those rocks . . ."

"You took the fall instead." Jamie fixed his eyes into hers. "You saved him, Jen."

"No, I was just along for the ride."

He took her hand. "We never did finish that lesson."

"I've fallen enough for a while."

"You got up."

"Think I can stay that way next time?"

"Depends if you do your homework," Jamie said and pulled a book out of the bag. "I didn't have time to wrap it."

Jen took the book in her free hand and read the title. "*Skiing Made Easy*?"

Jamie smiled. "You've got to start somewhere."

By
Mary Lane
Director—White Mountain Adaptive Ski School
Loon Mountain
Lincoln, New Hampshire

I have locked my door and chained myself to my computer in an effort to make myself write. Yesterday I had the same good intentions when two friends came to tell me the sun was shining . . . work could wait, the snow was melting . . . we had to ski. I think they used that same excuse two days before! So off we went and it was indeed a beautiful day for bumps—snow you could leave your mark in and no crowds to mess it up. We were having so much fun and skiing so well people were staring from the lift with that who-are-those-guys look! As much as I hate to admit it, the looks were for my companions: Geoff and David, two mono-skiers. The gawk factor is something you get used to when skiing with adaptive skiers; sometimes I think people will fall out of the lift turning to stare, trying to figure out how Ron skis so fast on one leg, or why John has riggers and two skis. You should see the looks when the mono- and bi-skiers go through the half pipe in the board park! That's what adaptive skiing is all about—no limits, no boundaries. There is no room on the mountain for any preconceived notion of the word "disability." When we ski, we're all fighting for balance; in an odd way that makes for a more level playing field.

My introduction to the world of "handicapped" skiing came in the 70s, while I was at college. I was required to do a

J-term* and I wanted to ski. My family had always skied at Haystack in Vermont, and fortunately for me they had one of the first "handicapped" ski programs. My proposal barely passed the professor's review committee, it smelled so much of "ski bum!" But a funny thing happened that first January: I fell in love with skiing all over again—or more specifically, with teaching skiing. So each January I submitted a different form of the same proposal and conned the head of the phys-ed department into acting as my mentor. Senior year I took a different tack, "A Photographic View of Winter," and again I skied. Most of my students were Vietnam vets. There were no sit-, mono-, or bi-skis back then. Most of my lessons were blind and 3T (three-tracking). My first blind student, Doug, and I skied together for a couple winters until we graduated to get "real jobs." So now I've come full circle—my real job is director of the adaptive ski program at Loon Mountain. I wonder what Doug's doing.

In the late 70s and early 80s, while I raised my three daughters, the "disabled" ski world made remarkable strides. I came back to teaching in the late 80s, missing the heyday of the sit-ski, but just in time to see the mono-ski take off and the bi-ski introduced. That's another great thing about this sport: There is still a lot of creating and inventing going on all over the country. Disabled Sports/USA is a national organization that promotes accessibility in sports from the beginner to the elite athlete. Each December they host the Ski Spectacular, a truly amazing event I've attended many times. My friend Bink went for the first time this year and wrote of her experience:

Our students all became our friends, and we talked
of life and shared our passion for skiing. We bloomed

*An independent project undertaken during the January break between first and second semesters.

as people, shared our personal triumphs over dinners, and realized the power we have as a cohesive group. The energy and powerful feelings we all felt couldn't be contained—we skied and danced and ate home-cooked meals with students, national examiners, equipment innovators, U.S. Disabled Ski Team members, and other instructors as if they were our close friends—because now they were! We realized we're all part of this huge organization that thrives on unbounded, unconditional love brought out through our passion for skiing. All our disabilities melted away, and our abilities shined. We learned that "we don't have problems, we have challenges."

So now it's the 90s. Ski schools are becoming snow sports schools in recognition of the different ways we dance down the mountain—on snowboards, snowblades, and telemark and alpine skis. This new way of thinking is good for the adaptive side of the sport, for we just bring different toys to the party. We tether the bi, guide the blind, speak with our hands, tinker with shocks and buckets for the mobility impaired, and break the standard teaching progressions into smaller bits so the developmentally delayed can join in the fun. *Hope Mountain* is fiction, but skiing for the disabled is a reality. Furthermore, the book's underlying message, that the benefits of sports go far beyond the sport itself, is the most remarkable aspect of all.